TH
GRE
ON EARTH?

THE LAST GREEN BOOK ON EARTH?

Judy Allen

Illustrated by
Martin Brown

To everyone who is trying to treat the
planet with some respect.

A Red Fox Book

Published by Random House Children's Books
20 Vauxhall Bridge Road, London SW1V 2SA

A division of Random House UK Ltd
London Melbourne Sydney Auckland
Johannesburg and agencies throughout the world

Text © Judy Allen 1994
Illustrations © Martin Brown 1994

Published by Red Fox 1994

1 3 5 7 9 10 8 6 4 2

This book is sold subject to the condition that it shall not, by way of trade or otherwise, be lent, resold, hired out, or otherwise circulated without the publisher's prior consent in any form of binding or cover other than that in which it is published and without a similar condition including this condition being imposed on the subsequent purchaser.

The rights of Judy Allen and Martin Brown to be identified as the author and illustrator of this work have been asserted by them in accordance with the Copyright, Designs and Patents Act, 1988.

Set in Caslon Roman by SX Composing Ltd, Rayleigh, Essex
Printed and bound in Great Britain by
Cox & Wyman, Reading, Berkshire

Random House UK Limited Reg No. 954009

ISBN 0 09 933711 8

The text paper used within this book is Alsaprint and is made in France from 100% recycled cellulose fibres. These fibres were deinked by the flotation method and bleached using hydrogen peroxide rather than any chlorine derivatives. The final product was improved by an optical brightening agent. All aqueous effluents were treated, prior to being returned to the river, in accordance with strict French regulations, and the by-products from the mill were non toxic.

CONTENTS

1	The facts of life	*1*
2	Why are there holes in the ozone layer?	*5*
3	Where are all the rainforests vanishing to?	*12*
4	When will the greenhouse effect begin?	*20*
5	How does rain become acid?	*26*
6	Who is polluting the rivers and seas?	*35*
7	Which are the most dangerous poisons?	*43*
8	What are we doing to other species?	*51*
9	End-of-term reports on industrial countries	*59*
10	And now for the good news . . .	*69*
11	Get clean	*76*
12	Get to look good	*82*
13	Get fed	*92*
14	Get rid . . .	*102*
15	Get switched on and revv'd up	*112*
16	Get away	*123*
17	Get green fingers	*130*
18	Get this!	*139*
19	What the stars say	*152*
20	What are we doing?	*159*
21	Is this the end?	*168*
Address list		*174*
Index		*182*

Acknowledgements

I am very grateful to Jeanne Griffiths and Patricia Moore for additional research and to Neil Verlander of Friends of the Earth whose comments on the final draft were invaluable.

Many thanks to Kate Petty for the original idea, and also to the following for advice, encouragement and information: Dr James Longhurst, Darren Hetherington and Paula Owen of the Atmospheric Research and Information Centre at Manchester Metropolitan University; Dr Simon Wolff of the Toxicology Department of University College Hospital, London; all at Friends of the Earth; all at Greenpeace; Anne Cahill and John Dalby of The Soil Association; The Consumers' Association, Alan Phillips of the Environmental Information Service; Tricia Barnett and Sue Wheat of Tourism Concern; and also to Population Concern, The Aluminium Can Recycling Campaign, WATCH Trust, British Hedgehog Preservation Society, Whale and Dolphin Conservation Society, Cyclist's Touring Club, Transport 2000, the Vegetarian Society and the staff at West Hill Reference Library, Wandsworth.

Chapter One

THE FACTS OF LIFE

The facts of life are quite straightforward as long as the story stops before it gets to the awkward part.

Amoebae divide, bees pollinate, plants seed, birds mate and lay eggs, the cat has kittens and – whoop-de-doo – we're up to the human chapter.

This is slightly more complicated because it goes beyond the technical bit, the who-puts-what-where bit. But apart from problems which are apparently rare in the rest of nature (like unwanted pregnancies and sexually transmitted diseases) there are all sorts of side issues, like what kind of deodorant should you use, and who pays on the first date.

But the awkward part – the really embarrassing part – the fact of life that no one wants to think about for too long – is this: If we don't begin to behave differently very soon, the planet may have to get rid of us in order to survive.

> "This is your planet speaking: green up or get off."

For one thing there are too many of us. For another we've never entirely grasped the fact that we're tenants of the Earth. We think of ourselves as owner-occupiers, which

1

means we assume we have the right to make changes. Since large numbers of us are clever, we also have the ability to do so. Since only very small numbers of us are wise, we are often surprised, not to say alarmed, when we pause to consider the changes we've made.

Some of these changes have been big and obvious, like remodelling the atmosphere, mixing poisonous chemicals with the water, and creating large areas of uninterrupted, easy-to-maintain desert.

Some have been relatively small, like extracting a mixture of liquid hydrocarbons from under the Earth's crust, blending in a compound of fluorine and chlorine, melding the lot into disposable plastic foam cups – and then complaining that we don't know how to throw them away.

Muttered warnings that things couldn't go on like this forever were first issued in the middle of the nineteenth century. By the late twentieth century the message was beginning to get through.

The United Nations organised a Conference on the Human Environment which was held at Stockholm in June 1972. Twenty years later, the UN organised another world conference, to take matters considerably further. This, a Conference on Environment and Development, with a much wider agenda, was held in Rio de Janeiro in June 1992. It was known as The Earth Summit.

> "For the first time in international politics we have consensus that the future of the planet is at stake if we do not reverse the process of abusing it." Maurice Strong, Secretary General of the Earth Summit. *Earth Summit 1992* (The Regency Press Corp, 1992)

The Earth Summit was attended by more than 10,000 delegates and 116 national political leaders from over 150 countries. A further 15,000 'concerned citizens and activists' participated in the parallel Global Forum, in the same city.

The Summit dealt with a vast range of subjects, including poverty and human health, the protection of the atmosphere, deforestation and the management of fragile ecosystems, conservation of biological diversity, sustainable agriculture, protection of oceans and freshwater supplies, safe management of toxic and hazardous wastes, and science for sustainable development.

There was at least one Summit cynic:

Ronnie Biggs, one-time train robber, broadcasting on his regular slot on Rio Radio: "Don't take your gold watch to the beach, it's too dangerous. Mind you, I wouldn't wear one to the conference either – there's probably bigger crooks there."

Many of the environmental pressure groups, though not cynical, were disappointed. It seemed there had been a lot of talk and not many results.

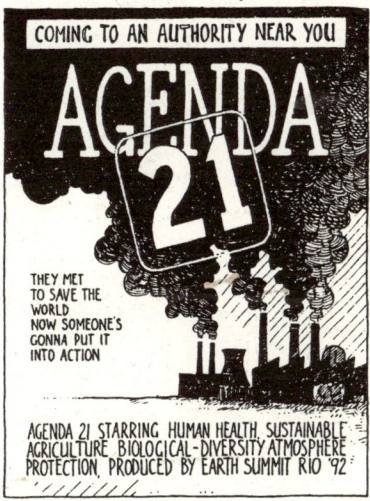

COMING TO AN AUTHORITY NEAR YOU

AGENDA 21

THEY MET TO SAVE THE WORLD NOW SOMEONE'S GONNA PUT IT INTO ACTION

AGENDA 21 STARRING HUMAN HEALTH, SUSTAINABLE AGRICULTURE, BIOLOGICAL-DIVERSITY ATMOSPHERE PROTECTION, PRODUCED BY EARTH SUMMIT RIO '92

However, one clear achievement was the establishment of Agenda 21. Agenda 21 is designed to create a practical plan of action to enable us and the-planet-as-we-know-it to survive into the twenty-first century. Now that there is an Agenda, there is a mechanism for checking progress. A dialogue, as they say, has been opened between world governments.

In his foreword to the official publication of the Earth Summit, Maurice Strong wrote: "It is up to all of us to build on the foundations laid by the Earth Summit to ensure that the decisions that have been taken at the global level be translated into national politics and practices at all levels."

At all levels. If you look at Section III, Chapter 28, of this same publication, you will find these words: "Each local authority should enter into a dialogue with its citizens, local organisations and private enterprises and adopt a local Agenda 21." The aim is to achieve this by 1996. The snag is that there are, as yet, no clear timetables for all this – and no decision about who will pay for it. However, it's still important to look out for your own local Agenda 21. Find out what the local authority plans to do. Find out what the local environmental groups plan to do.

This could be the best chance yet to change things. It would be a pity to miss it.

Chapter Two

WHY ARE THERE HOLES IN THE OZONE LAYER?

Partly because you want ice in your drink.

In 1985 the media released some information which was received with enormous surprise. It confirmed one of humanity's more far-reaching achievements. We had succeeded in creating a hole in the layer of ozone which had been hanging around in the lower stratosphere – largely unmolested – for several million years.

> *Stephen King, in his foreword to* Fear Itself, *published by Underwood & Miller (1990), wonders why it is that he is often asked "... to justify writing about ghosts and the walking dead in a nifty, modern world that is busy polluting all its water, depleting the ozone layer and strip mining arable land for coal so that there will never be an America that needs to face life without night basketball."*

In 1992 there was slightly less surprise, but a lot more anxiety, at the news that the hole over the Antarctic had increased in size until it was as large as the US and as deep as Mount Everest (confirmed by Japan's Meteorological Agency using data from NASA satellites and Antarctic research stations).

Also, although the different atmospheric conditions above the North Pole make the ozone layer less vulnerable there than it is above the South Pole, the threat of an eventual hole over the Arctic is very real.

In 1993, stratospheric ozone in the northern hemisphere reached an all-time low. It is likely to be lower still in 1994.

And so it goes on.

Looking back to 1985, it's difficult to grasp why the news came as such a shock. It was known as long ago as 1974 that the chlorine released by chlorofluorocarbons – CFCs – was destroying ozone. And by 1985 CFCs had been in use for more than 50 years (most famously to propel liquids out of aerosols and to cool fridges).

However, it turned out that most of the people who had been relying on CFCs to shoot spray into their armpits, or on to their hair, or at passing flies, didn't actually know the ozone layer existed until they'd already done their bit to damage it.

Ozone is a form of oxygen, but with a different molecular structure (three atoms per molecule instead of two) which is not good news at low levels, where it functions as a greenhouse gas (contributing to global warming) and is also one of the main ingredients of smog.

Up in the stratosphere, though, ozone filters the sunlight and cuts out a lot of the rays in the ultraviolet range.

Ultraviolet rays are responsible for the much-sought-after skin change known as sun-tanning. Unfortunately, large concentrations can cause the less popular skin changes known as cancer (and not only on human animals). They can also, among other things, kill off the minute sea organisms, which are the essential food of fish and sea mammals, and have a devastating effect on cereal crops.

When CFCs were developed (by the US chemical company, Du Pont) they were thought to be stable, and safe. At our level, they are. But release them into the air and they rise ever upwards until they reach the ozone layer. As they drift on up through it they meet the incoming ultraviolet rays, which react with them. The reaction causes the release of chlorine. And chlorine destroys ozone.

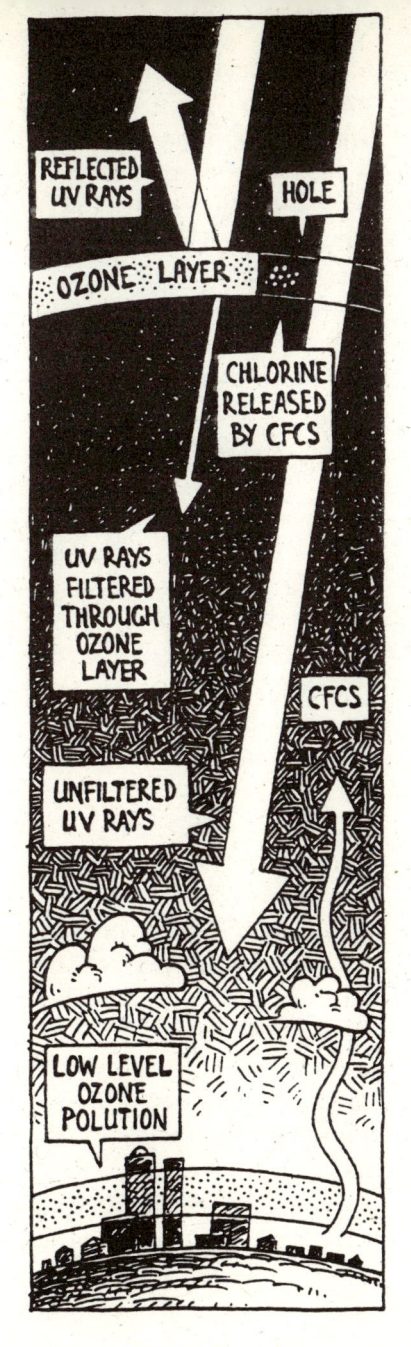

As the ozone layer is weakened and thinned, it lets in more ultraviolet radiation. So the destruction of the ozone layer is speeded up by ... the destruction of the ozone layer ...

The level of ozone in the lower stratosphere does vary naturally, but the CFC-attack has lowered the yearly average. This means that in some places the ozone veil thins out, forming a hole – not a precise hole with fixed edges but one that changes shape and size.

The governments of the developed countries have not always been famous for effective reactions to environmental warnings – but this one did get their attention.

The United Nations Environment Programme (UNEP) produced an international agreement to control ozone-depleting chemicals. This, the Montreal Protocol, was signed by more than twenty-four countries in 1986, and renegotiated in 1990.

By 1992 people in Europe and North America were getting fiercer warnings than usual on the subject of sun hats and barrier creams – and for a few days in the October of that year 50% of the ozone was lost over parts of South America. This encouraged the signatories of the Montreal Protocol to tighten it up in November 1992.

All this is very positive, but there is a snag.

Friends of the Earth estimate that for the chlorine in the stratosphere to get back to 1985-levels (which were already too high, hence the hole) by the year 2070, *all* use of the CFCs identified in the Montreal Protocol would need to have ceased by 1993.

However, the current agreement is to phase out the use of *most* CFCs by January 1996. And there are two distinct points of view on the phasing out of HCFCs (hydrofluorocarbons), which are CFC substitutes, and which have from 2% to 10% of the ozone depleting powers of CFCs. One says they should be phased out at the same rate as CFCs, certainly before the present projected date of 2003. The other says it is better to use HCFCs as a kind of stepping stone towards safer alternatives, to encourage industry to turn away from CFCs as soon as possible.

However you look at it, both kinds are damaging. It would therefore be an extremely good idea to stop using them – all of them – right now, if at all possible.

Aerosols are sometimes accused of being the main source, but few modern aerosols contain CFCs. (Exceptions include certain types of asthma inhaler. The National Asthma Campaign and the pharmaceutical industry are trying to find medically safe alternatives but, at the moment, babies and the desperately breathless who are not able to inhale for themselves still depend on CFCs to propel the medicine into their lungs.)

But CFCs are used in numerous other things – not all of which you have any direct control over.

As well as in fridges (in the insulating material in the walls and door and also in the coolant), they are used in air conditioners and for the precision-cleaning of delicate surfaces, such as optical glass and electronic circuit boards.

> The research department of one of the world's leading computer companies has finally come up with an electronic solvent that doesn't contain CFCs – it's called 'warm soapy water'.

They may be in the foam used to stuff furniture, in egg boxes and in take-away food cartons. They are often in stain removers, dry-cleaning fluid, shoe cleaners, dyes, adhesives and paint-on correcting fluids.

If you're using any of the last lot, read the labels. The name you're most likely to come across is 1.1.1-trichlorethan. This is methyl chloroform which is responsible for 13% of the chlorine in the lower stratosphere. It doesn't hang around as long as some of the other CFCs and so will clear sooner, but it's quite damaging enough. The signatories of the Montreal Protocol have agreed this should be phased out by January 1996 – but you can't start avoiding it too soon.

CFCs and HCFCs may be the most famous ozone-depleting chemicals, but they are not the only ones heavily in use.

Halon – used in fire-fighting equipment – is thought to be responsible for one quarter of the total ozone loss over Antarctica. This is a pity because Halon gas, pumped into burning engine rooms or computer rooms, starves the fire of oxygen, thus avoiding the use of messy and damaging water or foam.

The Montreal Protocol originally decreed that Halon should be phased out by the year 2000, but in November 1992 the date was brought forward to January 1994. (Researchers are working on alternatives, and there are plans to set up Halon-banks so that what is left can be stored safely and used only when essential.)

Carbon tetrachloride (used in pesticides, medicines and rubberised paints) and methyl chloroform (a solvent for cleaning metal and plastics) were originally to be phased out by the years 2000 and 2005 respectively. Both now have their limits set at January 1996.

So far there are no international controls on yet another ozone-enemy, methyl bromide (used to kill pests in stored crops and soil) even though it is already banned in the Netherlands where it was found to be poisoning the water.

Governments do seem to be trying to bring this particular horror story to an end, but it isn't easy. Alternatives are available but some of them are not all that ozone-friendly anyway – they still contain chlorine, even though to a lesser degree. Of those which don't contain chlorine, and don't damage the ozone layer, many manage to contribute to the greenhouse effect, instead.

Also, vast numbers of people already believe themselves to be totally dependant on these things. And in the developing countries there are vast numbers more, keen to have the chance to become dependent.

This raises one more crucial point. Having cheerfully filled the air with CFCs and all the rest for the past fifty years, it would be totally unreasonable for Europe and North America to frown on the ambitions of the developing countries. Pretty well every household in the developed countries has a fridge – some have more than one. If we think they're such a great idea (one ice cube or two?) what right have we to try to deprive other people? Why should they like rancid food any more than we do?

The pressure from the Montreal Protocol – and the fact that there are a surprising number of scientists who do actually care about the environment – means that acceptable alternatives are being found. However, they are more expensive to produce. So if the rich countries want the poor countries to accept them, then the rich countries must make funds available.

Meanwhile, those of us who live in the greedy nations must be willing to use less. It isn't always necessary to wait for the official bans to come into force – it's often possible to apply personal bans at once.

Personal bans

You've probably already stopped using unacceptable aerosols. The next step might be to pay attention to the labelling on stain removers, shoe cleaners, adhesives etc and try to avoid the ones with ozone-destroyers in them.

Don't worry too much about the fridge – it isn't crouching menacingly in the corner of the kitchen planning to destroy the sky. The CFCs are only released during its manufacture and when it's thrown away, not when it's in operation. If the household is planning to invest in a new one, use whatever influence you have to make sure they buy green (a couple of companies are already making CFC-free models, and they'll be commonplace quite soon). Also, check that whoever is taking away the old one will remove and recycle the CFCs in the coolant. Sometimes the retailer supplying the new fridge can guarantee to dispose of the old one properly – if not, the local dump may be equipped to do this, or else the local council will usually do the honours.

If you have a Halon fire extinguisher (maybe in the car) ask the local fire brigade for advice on what to use instead.

And don't feel threatened by every sunny day. Sunhats, sunglasses and sunblocking creams have always been a good idea, it's just that now they're an even better idea than they used to be, especially if you have pale skin.

> "The coldness of Antarctic air permits the formation of Polar Stratospheric Clouds (PSCs) composed of particles of nitric acid trihydrate and this formation removes active forms of nitrogen (which would 'tie up' active forms of chlorine and prevent ozone destruction) and also provides a surface for chemical reactions, transforming chlorine from hydrochloric acid (HCl) or chlorine nitrate ($ClONO_2$) into active molecular chlorine (Cl_2). Cl_2 is broken down by ultraviolet light, leaving chlorine atoms (Cl) which react with nitrogen dioxide (NO_2) to recreate chlorine nitrate ($ClONO_2$). When this reacts on the PSCs, the process begins again." Based on information from the Stratospheric Ozone Review Group supplied by Friends of the Earth.

Chapter Three
WHERE ARE THE RAINFORESTS VANISHING TO?

Into lavatory seats and executive desks, among other places.

If Ronald Reagan had been right when he said, "eighty per cent of pollution is caused by plants and trees," we would not have a problem.

The greater part of the temperate forests of Europe and North America were lost before living memory. Trees in the rich northern countries continue to be felled – for timber and to clear land for development.

Half the band of rich equatorial forest which circles the globe has gone, too. The rest is being lost at the rate of 160,000 square kilometres a year. If we continue as we are going we could be down to about one-tenth of the original by the middle of the twenty-first century.

It's hard to know why the then US President's statement should have come out back to front – possibly he was looking in a mirror at the time. In fact, trees absorb carbon dioxide, one of the principal greenhouse gases, and keep it locked within. (It is released when the tree dies and rots or when it is felled and burned.)

His successor, George Bush, understood the importance of trees, and, at the Earth Summit in Rio, remarked that the tropical forests function as a sink for carbon dioxide. Although technically true, this went down extremely badly with the developing countries.

What the US seemed to be saying was that if the South would only protect its forests, then the power stations, factories and cars of the North could continue to spew out unlimited quantities of CO_2.

> *"I think everything is going sadly wrong with the world. Everyone knows about the ozone layer but there's so many other things going on. We've abused the world so much."* Gary Barlow (from 'Take That',) talking to Smash Hits *magazine.*

It is moderately obvious that the rich countries of the North are astonishingly unfair to the poorer or developing countries of the South. What may be less obvious is that they are unfair in such complicated ways.

The rich countries have never hesitated to exploit natural resources – oil, coal, wood, precious metals and whatever else is available. That is largely how they got rich. They are also fond of planting their money like seeds in investments, so that it grows.

In the oil boom of the 1970s the Organization of Petroleum Exporting Countries (OPEC) planted enormous sums of money in various banks, including in Britain's Famous Four – Barclays, Lloyds, Midland and NatWest.

In order to make this money earn its keep, the banks offered loans, at low interest rates, to Third World countries – which were rich in natural resources, including rainforests, but not in cash.

The money was intended for equipment and road-building projects to make it easier to get at these natural resources and then to export them. The revenue earned from the exports was supposed to enable the borrowers to pay off the interest on these debts and still make a reasonable living. (You will notice that the creditors were expecting to do quite nicely, too.)

The plan began to go wrong when complications in the world economy caused interest rates to rise sharply and market prices for numerous Third World exports (coffee, for example, and sugar) to fall dramatically.

"The debt owed by poor developing countries to their rich Northern creditors now amounts to a staggering one thousand three hundred billion US dollars." Friends of the Earth.

Under pressure to repay debts that were growing steadily larger the Third World countries struggled to increase their exports – among them the tropical hardwoods ... mahogany, teak, sapele ...

Naturally not all the money paid for the timber reached those who were felling and selling. Much was absorbed by dealers and other middlemen. These people are useful – essential, even – but frequently cream off more than

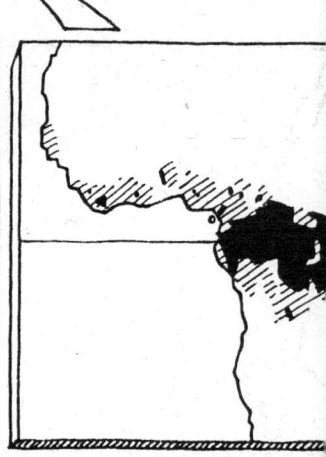

fig I... the plan

fig II. the reality

is fair or reasonable. Chris Cox of the Ecological Trading Company (which deals only in timber cut according to good forestry practice, and which ensures that fair prices are paid) has said: "In Ecuador, a tree whose timber can sell for $4,000 retail (about £2,000) in the UK is sold locally for as little as $6 (about £3)."

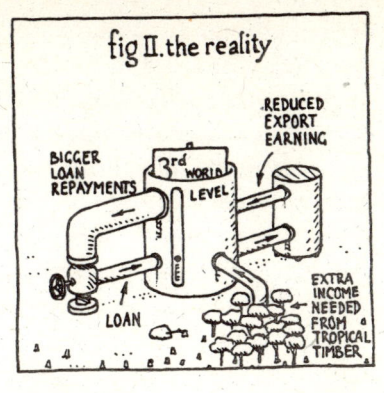

Timber is not the only exploitable resource in a rainforest. Vast tracts have also been devastated in order to extract valuable minerals – iron, copper, gold, diamonds and oil. Other expanses of forest have been swept aside to establish cattle ranches for cheap meat and plantations for cash crops of bananas, cocoa, vanilla and so on. These are almost never a good idea.

Rainforest trees take most

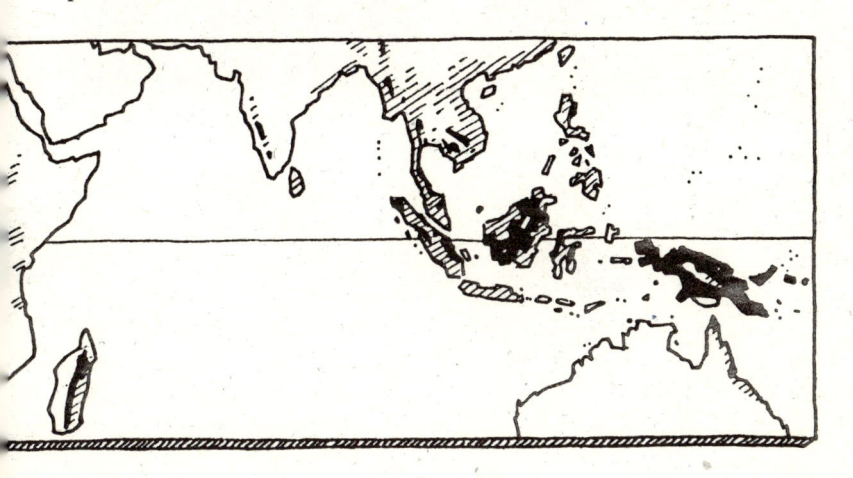

of the nutrients out of the soil, only returning them when they die and rot down. If the trees are removed, the starved and easily-eroded soil cannot support other vegetation for long. The grazing is meagre and soon gone and the crops can only be sustained with massive quantities of fertilisers. Small farmers discovered this reality generations ago, which is why they continually slash and burn fresh patches for their crops. The charcoal from the burned trees enriches the soil briefly (meanwhile, of course, carbon dioxide is released into the atmosphere, adding to the problem of global warming). Similarly, the ranches and plantations have to move on to fresh forest.

The rich North watched in horror as huge areas of rainforest disappeared – whole species of animal, plant and insect were lost – and the soil, no longer held in place by the tree roots, was washed away by the rain in devastating mud slips. The North was – and is – hugely critical of this mismanagement of the rainforests. It maintains that they are a global resource which must be preserved.

At the same time, the North continues to expect repayment of the ever-increasing debt. It is slow to suggest how anyone is supposed to repay the debt without, in effect, rapidly pulling the forest to bits and selling it. When it comes to writing off the debt, or at least reducing it, slow has turned to dead slow – although Britain, Canada, the former West Germany and the US have at last cancelled some of the debts owed by the poorest countries.

> "The World Bank have calculated that 'hard core' poverty almost doubled in Ivory Coast as a result of austerity measures designed to promote debt repayment. This country's rainforest is being lost at a rate of over 15 per cent per year, the highest rate in the world." Friends of the Earth

It is not true, however, that the countries of the North do nothing but take money away from the South. They also supply financial aid. Sometimes this is helpful – but sometimes it goes tragically wrong.

An example: aid-money is granted to fund the establishment of a sustainable timber plantation, complete with trees and sawmills. The thinking behind this is that fast-growing timber, eucalyptus perhaps, can be planted and then harvested with clear consciences and no serious damage. It sounds so simple.

What can happen next is simple, too. Primary rainforest is cut and cleared to make way for the plantation.

Britain is among the countries which supply aid – doubtless with the best of intentions – and which speak earnestly about the importance of saving what is left of the rainforests. Yet Britain is a major importer of tropical hardwoods, and does OK out of the VAT levied on these imports.

> "In 1992/3, the British Government gave £28m for forestry projects. It earned five times this amount on the VAT from sales of tropical timber."
> Friends of the Earth

There is more.

Brazilian mahogany is being cut illegally from Indian forest reserves – and a sizeable percentage of this is sold to Britain. The Philippines, struggling to protect their share of the forest belt, have banned the export of logs and raw timber. Inevitably, illegal logging goes on there, too. Britain does not have a corresponding import ban on this timber, so some of it reaches British markets without hindrance.

Here it is made not only into lavatory seats, executive desks and expensive furniture, but also into more mundane things, like door and window frames, plywood, planks and boards. (However, if you find you have some of this material already, on no account drag it out and burn it in disgust. Value and respect it – just make sure it's the last piece of its kind you ever own.)

Meanwhile, back in the forest, sustainable development is possible (although many of the forest tribes who understand this are themselves in danger of extinction).

Brazil nuts, for example, cannot be grown on plantations because the bees who pollinate the flowers are also dependent on a species of wild orchid. The right set-up exists only in undamaged parts of the forest. Honey, wild fruits, medicinal plants, resins, sisal, bamboo, raffia and vegetable dyes can all be collected without impoverishing the environment, so long as they are harvested with due care and not simply plundered. Rubber, too, because the trees are tapped and 'milked', not felled or damaged. (Not that rubber production is without its dangers – local workers are sometimes exploited and heavy production can lead to destructive road-building.)

It is even possible to take limited amounts of timber, from suitable areas, using small, portable sawmills which can be manoeuvred within the forest without the need for roads or heavy machinery. The highly-principled Ecological Trading Company has proved this in Peru. (Also, they pay a proper price on the forest floor, which means that the timber producers can actually afford to care for their area of forest.)

Even so, it's preferable only to take these things from the periphery. If demand rises so that people are encouraged to search deeper in the forest, then eventually roads will be built and there will be more and more outside contact with forest Indians. This carries all kinds of risks for them – from unbalancing their long-established societies, to passing on infectious diseases which have never been encountered before.

"Warner Brothers Studios (in Hollywood) has officially announced that it will no longer use rainforest plywood for set construction and other studios are expected to follow suit shortly."
Green Magazine, *(May 1993)*

There are other dangers, too.

Campaigns conducted in the rich countries are extremely important, but also – for most of us – relatively easy. Wear the t-shirt, buy the Brazil nuts, avoid the tropical hardwoods, write letters of protest to banks and governments. At tree-roots level, though, the experience can be rather more vivid. In 1988 Chico Mendes, leader of the Brazilian rubber-tappers and highly-respected pioneer of sustainable development in the Amazon, was assassinated by two local ranchers. The men were convicted and imprisoned in 1990, but escaped early in 1993.

Plants, including some with medicinal properties, destroyed ... species upon species of animal lost forever ... thousands of people deprived of their normal lifestyle ... others violently deprived of life itself.

Does anyone need a glossy, executive-style mahogany lavatory seat *that* much?

> It is estimated that rainforests once covered 16 million square kilometres and are now down to 8 million square kilometres. Approximately 160,000 square kilometres are being destroyed annually, with a further 150,000 square kilometres (in Amazonia) under threat of flooding as a side effect of the building of hydro-electric dams.

Chapter Four
WHEN WILL THE GREENHOUSE EFFECT BEGIN?

It probably already has.

If you're talking greenhouses, we live in one anyway, that's why the planet can support life – for now.

The Earth is warmed mainly by the heat-energy from the sun bouncing back off the surface. The direct rays don't do much more than take the chill off. (That's why, when you climb above sea level towards the sun, you get colder rather than hotter – unless, of course, you succeed in reaching the stratosphere, in which case you will warm up again.)

Life on earth needs greenhouse gases. If they were not there to trap heat-energy, it would all escape. This would result in an alarming overall global temperature drop of approximately thirty degrees centigrade. They also trap the moisture evaporating from seas, rivers, etc, which forms clouds, and then rains back down again; clearly a useful effect.

Greenhouse gases (carbon dioxide, methane, nitrous oxides and surface ozone) occur naturally. We didn't make the lot from scratch.

Naturally occurring carbon dioxide (CO_2) emerges when animals (human or otherwise) breathe out. It also comes from rotting organic material.

Naturally occurring methane (CH_4) is given off by flatulence and decomposing organic matter, including vegetation rotting in swamps and marshes. (Methane is also known as marsh gas. This is what causes the erratic will o' the wisp lights which unwise travellers sometimes decide to follow – usually just before becoming totally lost and sinking.)

Naturally occurring nitrous oxide (N_2O) comes from human and animal excreta.

Naturally occurring surface ozone, which is a form of oxygen with a different molecular structure (three atoms instead of two) is created by the reaction on oxygen of ultraviolet radiation or of an electrical discharge – lightning, for example.

To keep the natural theme going, naturally occurring greenhouse gases are also removed naturally. For example, carbon dioxide is taken out of the atmosphere, as part of the carbon cycle, by all green plants, from giant redwoods to phytoplankton. They photosynthesize it into nourishment (carbon) and give off oxygen. It is also absorbed by the oceans.

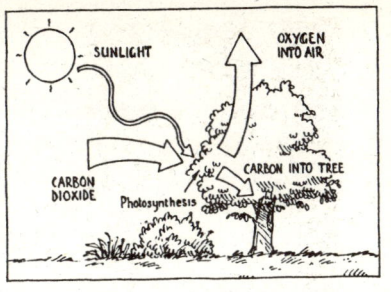

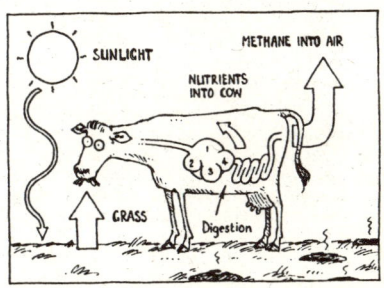

The Earth and its atmosphere co-existed in a reasonably balanced state (with a few wild fluctuations) for some thousands of millions of years. But then we started to manufacture the greenhouse gases in ever-increasing amounts. We also began to destroy enormous amounts of the vegetation that used to sop up the surplus. We did not, at first, know that this was a bad idea. Some of us still don't.

> "The most important thing about Spaceship Earth – an instruction book didn't come with it." R. Buckminster Fuller. Geological guru of 1960s

The large portion of carbon dioxide which is created entirely by human endeavour comes from the burning of wood and fossil fuels; it emerges from the chimneys of factories and power stations and the exhaust pipes of vehicles, including aircraft.

Some of the extra methane is also generated by the burning of wood, coal and oil. Some seeps out from the rubbish buried in huge landfill sites and from the marsh-like rice paddies. And some comes from the four gaseous stomachs of the cattle we breed in such large numbers.

The nitrous oxides are topped up by the burning of wood and fossil fuels and by the extensive use of fertilisers.

Additional surface ozone is manufactured at an alarming rate by the chemical reaction of sunlight on the hydrocarbons and nitrous oxides in vehicle exhausts. (The output from the developed countries has increased by more than 60% in the last thirty years.)

Up in the stratosphere, ozone is essential. At lower levels it is not only a contributor to global warming but also toxic at concentrations above 0.1 parts per million (not hard to achieve in a traffic jam on a hot day).

(The belief in ozone as a healthy and invigorating ingredient of fresh air came about because its presence – in safe amounts – can be detected by its distinctive smell near the sea and after thunderstorms. Also, in natural circumstances, it is highly reactive and quick to drop the third atom and turn back into oxygen – which accounts for the fact that the air is often genuinely purer after a storm or on a clifftop.)

As long ago as 1896, a Swedish chemist, Svante Arhenius, warned that human activities could be responsible for the gradual warming of the planet. Increasingly urgent warnings have been issued, on a regular basis, ever since. Responses have been mixed, but not usually especially encouraging. Disbelief has always featured among them.

In fact a weird new balance is developing. The damage to the ozone layer is reducing the speed of the rise in temperature, and the sulphur pollution from burning coal and oil is also cooling the atmosphere slightly. So it is actually possible that the greenhouse effect will increase as the ozone-destroyers are reduced.

However, unless we are happy with the effects of unfiltered ultraviolet radiation and acid rain, this balance is not a useful one.

It does show, though, that global atmosphere is so vast and the issues so complex that no one can be one hundred per cent certain of precisely what is happening now, let alone one hundred per cent certain of what will happen in the future.

The dynamics of the atmosphere are not fully understood. Eminent scientists issue warnings. Other (fewer) eminent scientists issue reassurances.

What is certain is that the overall temperature of the planet is now between 0.03 and 0.06 degrees higher than it was before the Industrial Revolution, and that the overall temperature rose by 0.5 degrees in the century between 1890 and 1990.

If the warming continues at

> "We know the greenhouse gases are capable of trapping heat in the atmosphere; we know that atmospheric concentrations of these gases are soaring (confirmed by the Intergovernmental Panel on Climate Change, based on studies of the Vostok ice core in Antarctica). The debate centres on a key uncertainty – exactly how much the temperatures will go up in consequence, and what the response of the climate system will be." Greenpeace

its present rate – or faster – there are some obvious consequences. We have read about them often. The polar ice caps, which are already shrinking, will melt more rapidly, sea levels will rise, and there will be severe coastal flooding (coast to coast flooding in low-lying countries). There will also be major and unpredictable climate changes (including high drama in the form of windstorms, floods, tornadoes and droughts). Climate changes will affect food crops and may well threaten the survival of numerous plant and animal species.

It is true that the planet's temperature has undergone drastic changes before – in the ice ages for example – but these came about gradually, giving plants and animals a chance to adapt or move. (Or, in some cases, opt out and die.) Global warming is already, in planetary terms, very rapid.

Scientists like to be 99% certain of their facts before they make pronouncements. Although it seems likely that the certainty-quotient of the majority of those working in the relevant sciences is close to 90%, they still speak cautiously.

We could wait to take action until the whole body of scientific opinion has topped up its certainty-factor by the missing few percent. By then, though, the problems will be ten polluting years greater, the ill effects ten destructive years harsher, and recovery further away and more difficult – if not totally impossible – to achieve.

It hardly seems worth the risk of waiting.

At the Earth Summit at Rio, the United States held out on the subject of the reduction of carbon dioxide emissions until the wording was watered down (no binding legislation, just a general agreement that all the signatories would try harder). They were worried that, because most of the emissions come from industry and cars, a major reduction would inevitably mean loss of revenue and jobs.

They were also under huge pressure from the extremely

> "We cannot permit the extreme in the environment to shut down the United States. We cannot shut down the lives of many Americans by going to the extreme on the environment." President George Bush, *Earth Summit 1992* (The Regency Press Corp, 1992)

powerful oil, coal and automobile industries, who like to see profits rising.

The Mega-Maxi-Multinational Corporations Inc of this world are not receptive to warnings. They just mutter about scaremongering. They don't wish to know that New York, London and Tokyo will eventually be drowned if global warming continues to melt ice at its present rate. It's strange they won't listen, because the people who run them are almost certainly human and just as likely to get wet, hungry and fried as anyone else.

One fact that might get them interested, though, is that studies in Australia, Europe and North America all indicate that excessive CO_2 emissions are the result of inefficient use of power and that it actually makes fine economic sense to reduce them – even if for no other reason.

The worst case scenario is best not thought about.

The best case scenario is that natural mechanisms will come into action in time to counteract the greenhouse effect.

In the meantime, there is plenty that governments – and individuals – can do to cut down on the production of greenhouse gases. It must, surely, be worth a little inconvenience to make sure that life, with all its evolving and diversifying and developing and seeding and growing and pupating and creating, continues on Earth.

> Incoming solar energy travels in the form of short wavelength radiations. These can penetrate the Earth's atmosphere (which protects it from the deadly cold of outer space). The atmosphere itself absorbs about ¼, deflects ¼ back out into space, and deflects another ¼ on to the surface. The rest reaches the surface directly (and 3% is bounced back out again). When the received energy returns from earth it travels in longer wavelengths, in the infra-red part of the spectrum. Clouds and water vapour, with carbon dioxide and other greenhouse gases in the atmosphere, absorb this radiation. The absorption warms the lower atmosphere.

Chapter Five

HOW DOES RAIN BECOME ACID?

By mingling with the gases of the burning past.

I'VE ONLY LOST AN EAR AND SOME TEETH.. FRANK, ROUND THE CORNER IS COMPLETELY GONE...

All rain is usually slightly acid – unless it contains particles of calcium and magnesium which may make it alkaline.

Acidic rain can wear away rock and stone, given time, not just by beating against it but by eating into it, until the carvings on cathedrals seem to be melting down, and the columns on great buildings look like half-sucked sticks of rock. The gases which create the acid content include sulphur dioxide and nitrogen oxides from natural and man-made emissions.

However, since the Industrial Revolution, some rain has been considerably more acid than usual.

The term 'acid rain' was first used in 1852, by Robert Angus Smith, who was studying air pollution around Manchester. It is still used – but in fact the approved title for the phenomenon is 'acid deposition'.

There are two kinds of acid deposition.

There is dry deposition, in which the pollution is deposited, more or less unchanged, in the form of a gas or soot. Dry deposition does most of its damage near its source.

There is also wet deposition, which includes rain, snow, hail, fog and mist. The pollutants involved in wet deposition go through various atmospheric chemical reactions and changes. Unlike the dry kind, this travels far and wide, causing damage both directly (by acidifying streams, rivers and lakes) and indirectly (by causing further chemical reactions in soil and water, which in turn trigger the release of toxic heavy metals, such as aluminium).

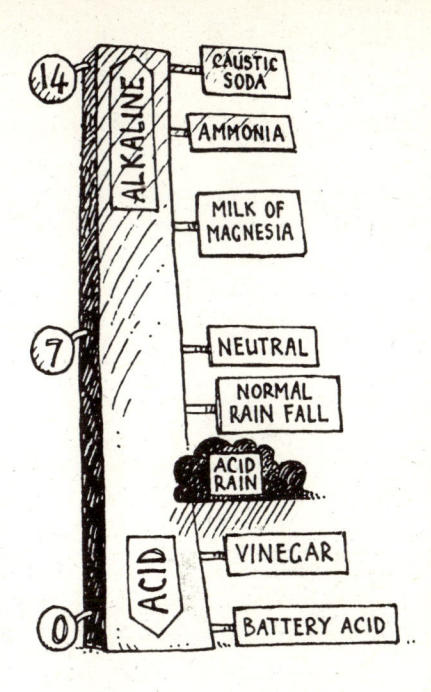

Acidity is measured by counting the number of hydrogen ions in any given liquid solution. The presence of hydrogen ions indicates the solution is acid, the presence of hydroxil ions indicates that it is alkaline. As the relative quantity of hydrogen and hydroxil ions is constant, a measure of the one automatically reveals the measure of the other. It is usual to measure both acidity and alkalinity on a logarithmic scale, the pH scale, which specifically expresses the number of hydrogen ions.

The scale runs from 0, the most acidic (eg battery acid), to 14, the most alkaline (eg caustic soda). A pH of 7 indicates neutral, while normal rainfall usually has a pH of between 5 and 6.

If water from lake, river or stream shows a reading below pH5, then it is more than probable that acid deposition is present.

The key pollutants which constitute acid deposition are sulphur dioxide (SO_2) and nitrogen oxides (NO_x), (though ozone (O_3), non-methane volatile organic compounds (NMVOCs) and ammonia (NH_3) can also play a part in the complex chemistry).

Sulphur dioxide and nitrogen oxides are formed by burning the sulphur and nitrogen naturally present in fossil fuels. Once formed, they react with water (present in the air even when it isn't raining) to create acidity.

Ozone occurs naturally and is also created artifically by the reactions between nitrogen oxides and hydrocarbons (a compound of hydrogen and carbon released by burning coal, oil and petrol) and between nitrogen oxides and NMVOCs.

NMVOCs are produced mainly by industrial processes and solvents, and ammonia (NH_3) comes from animal urine and excreta and reaches its highest concentrations around heavily farmed areas.

When the early factories and power stations were found to be choking the industrial towns which surrounded them, the decision was made to build their chimneys higher, to take the smoke up, up and away. This made life better around the factories themselves. Unfortunately, though, the emissions didn't just disperse in the atmosphere, as had been expected, they travelled on the wind until they were deposited in distant rural areas – or other countries.

Exactly where all this unappealing stuff ends up depends on which way the wind blows.

Because of the prevailing winds, Britain doesn't 'import' much more than 12% of its acid deposition from other countries.

The four Scandinavian countries, on the other hand,

get almost all of theirs from abroad, quite a lot of it from Britain. Information from Norway, in particular, suggests that about 90% of their acid rain comes from other countries, that 80-90% of acid damage is due specifically to sulphur, and that the largest 'exporter' of sulphur to Norway is Britain, with Germany close behind. Once again, we have been caught out in our mistaken belief that things can be thrown away, or blown away by the wind. We thought 'away' meant 'nowhere'. In fact, of course, 'away' is simply somewhere else.

The United Nations Economic Commission for Europe (UN-ECE) has set up a Coordinating Centre for Effects (CCE) in the Netherlands which, among other things, produces maps showing the areas most at risk; that is, not just those which receive the highest dosages of acidity, but also those least able to survive the onslaught. The areas shown to be suffering are very widespread, including Western Britain, the whole of Scandinavia and the

> "I'd like to make people understand we must stop looking for other planets and take care of the one we already have. The world must be seen as a whole; what happens in one country can affect all the rest." Pernille van Grieken, 15, Norway

mountainous regions of central Europe.

In order to determine which areas are most at risk from wet deposition, 'critical loads' have to be assessed. A critical load is defined as the amount of acid deposition any given area can take without permanent environmental damage. The critical load for sulphur deposition depends at least partly on how rapidly the soil can neutralise the acid.

A CRITICAL LOAD

On soft, porous base-rock, like chalk or limestone, the acid is neutralised. On hard base-rock, such as granite, it is not. And in places where the soil is naturally acid – upland areas and peat bogs for example – the addition of acid deposition can be desperately destructive.

It is harder to define the critical load for nitrogen because its action is more complex. It doesn't only cause acidification, it also causes eutrophication (or over-fertilisation).

Nitrogen is vital to the chain of life. It forms an essential part of protein and it is the main component of air. It is absorbed by green plants, which are then eaten by animals, which eventually excrete the nitrogen back into the environment.

Over-fertilisation may not sound like a problem, but it is. Over-stimulated plants and trees may outgrow the ability of their environment to support them. This, in turn, will mean that the plants (and especially the trees) will be under too much stress to cope with setbacks – like temporary drought, for example.

The suddenly enriched vegetation is also likely to use up more than its share of natural nutrients from the soil, reducing the soils own ability to cope with acidification. And, if there is more nitrogen than the plant growth can take up, the surplus will stay in the soil, acidifying it. The problem is always worse in winter when plants are not taking in nourishment and the nitrogen has a chance to build up.

> In 1993, the Swedish and Norwegian Clean Air Campaigners noted "critical loads for acidity are now being exceeded over three-quarters of Europe."

When airborne pollutants in gas form are being considered, the term used is not 'critical loads' but 'critical levels'. Here, calculations are usually made on the effects of each individual pollutant. However, pollutants almost never make solo appearances, and certain mixtures cause far more damage together than the sum of the damage caused by each on its own. For safety's sake, it is usually wise to regard all figures as underestimates.

Lakes, plants, trees and buildings – all are at risk to some degree or another.

> "In Sweden, 90,000km of rivers and 18,000 lakes have been affected, mainly by acid rain carried by the wind from Britain and other European countries." Greenpeace

An acidified lake may look quite beautiful, clear and clean. But it is only clear because it is empty, its waterlife killed off. Salmon and trout, in particular, can't cope with high acidity – nor can frogs, nor the larvae of many insects. The knock-on effect of the loss of fish and insect larvae is the loss of the animals – including otters and ospreys – which once fed on them.

Peat bogs, which are already naturally acid, are particularly vulnerable. The effect on flowering plants and crops is still being studied – but it is already clear that the ones in granite areas or on poor soil are suffering.

All building materials are affected, but those which sustain most damage are sandstone, brick, marble and limestone. Lime neutralises the acidity but has to break down and blend with it in order to do so. (The run-off from acid-eroded limestone will have a higher pH value than the rain that fell on it originally.)

Acid in groundwater can even corrode copper pipes.

Although there is some controversy about whether or not acid rain is the direct cause of tree-death in Britain, it is generally agreed that it reduces the ability of trees to cope with disease, insect attack and other problems, so its indirect effect is not disputed.

There is no doubt that acid deposition is both a direct and an indirect cause of tree-death in Europe and Scandinavia. Coniferous trees are especially susceptible – they don't drop their leaves annually and so they retain the acidity for longer. It is becoming increasingly common for us to see examples of die-back, where the top of the tree, which gets the full force of the acid deposition, is starkly dead, though the rest appears to be healthy.

Also, none of this polluted air is good to breathe.

There are various possible courses of action.

One, which is being used quite extensively in Scandinavia, is to introduce lime (calcium carbonate, $CaCO_3$) to lakes to neutralize the acidity. There are various ways of doing this, including mixing it with water into a slurry that can be sprayed, scattering it by hand into the streams that feed the lakes, or dropping pellets from helicopters. Liming has been shown to improve conditions for salmon, trout and some other forms of water life.

On the negative side, it has to be said that it is a very expensive process, not at all practical in remote areas and that it changes the chemistry of the water in ways that are not yet fully understood. Since the areas suffering most from acid deposition are usually those which had some natural acidity anyway, liming them is likely to throw their whole ecology out of balance.

A better solution would be to reduce the emissions of sulphur dioxide and nitrogen oxide at source. Creating more fuel-efficient cars would

"In an area of 7000 square miles (11265km) in southern Norway almost all fresh water fish are extinct. The cost for liming Norwegian rivers and lakes will be 20-30 million pounds per year." The Committee of County Councillors Against Acid Rain in the Agder and Telemark counties of Norway

help. So would fitting all cars with catalytic converters which reduce the amount of pollutants they blow out. And so, of course, would the simple expedient of using cars far, far less.

When it comes to the emissions from power stations, factories and home heating systems, the sulphur content of the coal and oil used can be reduced by processing. New-style more efficient boilers and furnaces produce less of the nitrogen oxides, and the addition of limestone to furnaces (not always possible at the moment) can also reduce the amount of sulphur dioxide given off in the smoke.

At a seminar in Göteborg, Sweden, in April 1992, twenty European non-Governmental environmental organisations (NGOs), agreed that overall reductions (that is to say, more reductions from heavy pol-

luters, less from light polluters) needed to be 90% in the case of sulphur dioxide and nitrogen oxide, and 75% volatile organic compounds, ammonia and tropospheric ozone (which last would be achieved by reducing the nitrogen oxides and volatile organic compounds).

It's easy to put all the blame on power stations and industry, but it's extremely important to remember that they are only there because we want them. In the end, it seems that this complex and serious problem must be attacked on all sides at once – by improved technology which can reduce emissions at source – by judicious liming where appropriate – and by our willingness to cut down on the things we think we need.

What we all have to do is to be less wasteful of the energy that supplies light, heat and the power to run computers and washing machines – to depend less on cars – and to demand fewer of the products the industrial processes are making.

And that is the acid truth.

> In 1990, the Department of the Environment noted the following chief sources of the acid deposition pollutants: SO_2 principally from coal-burning power stations, and NO_x principally from road transport (which is also responsible for some of the SO_2 and most of the carbon monoxide emissions). It also admitted that, of every country in Western Europe, Britain produces the most SO_2.

Chapter Six

WHO IS POLLUTING THE RIVERS AND SEAS?

Just about everyone, directly or indirectly.

The traditional figure of the sea-god Poseidon, wielding his trident, is beginning to look more and more like an oceanic park-keeper, hoping to pick up three pieces of rubbish at once.

Twenty-five years ago, people crossing the Atlantic or the Pacific by yacht, raft or catamaran reported regular sightings of litter, even at the farthest possible points from land. The situation has not improved since.

Once, the waters of the world seemed deep enough to swallow whatever we cared to dump in them. Sadly, though, we over-estimated their capacity. Or possibly we underestimated our own ability to create waste.

Either way, we've overdone it – but it's extremely difficult to stop.

The Global Environmental monitoring system, sponsored by the UN, lists 158 heavily polluted rivers.

Most of the water flowing in Poland's river Vistula is too contaminated *even* to be used by industry.

Efforts are being made to clean some of these waterways. The Indian government, for example, has set aside massive funds to help the Ganges.

In some places, though, authorities still need a lot of persuading to take action. They remain convinced that most rivers are fast enough and deep enough to dilute the pollution, and it's difficult to make them rethink.

Pollutants reach rivers in a variety of ways.

One source is the run-off of silage liquor (from fermented grass), slurry (liquid manure) and chemicals from agricultural land. These chemicals include poisons (pesticides) and nutrients (fertilisers). It's obvious what poison does, but too many nutrients are almost as harmful because they overfeed algae. Algae are simple aquatic plant forms, which range from one-celled microorganisms to large flabby seaweeds. Overfed, they multiply into massive algae blooms – which sound rather attractive, but which choke streams and rivers and use up the oxygen so that other waterlife dies.

Another source is the run-off from city streets, with all the dust, rubbish and lead from vehicle exhausts that flows with it.

A third is 'leachate', which can also blight aquifers and other underground water supplies. It is made up of water mixed with all the results of the corrosion, putrefaction and general corruption that goes on in landfill rubbish sites. Eventually it seeps out to taint whatever it touches – and its tendency to flow downhill frequently leads it to streams or rivers.

A fourth is noxious waste discharged directly into rivers from factories along their banks; a fifth is domestic waste of all kinds which reaches the river via sewage treatment works. In with the more obvious domestic wastes are heavy-duty household cleaners and bleaches, together with phosphates (from washing powders and liquids) which feed algae.

(Don't get too depressed at this stage. For one thing, the story is going to get worse, so you may as well keep some depression in reserve. For another, there is every chance that it will get better, given enough commonsense, goodwill, canny technology and suitable funding.)

To continue – anything that goes into rivers generally ends up in the sea, sometimes caught at the mouths of estuaries, sometimes swilling around the coastlines, sometimes much further out.

The belief that pollutants would be diluted so much that they would effectively vanish has turned out to be an illusion. PCBs (polychlorinated biphenyls), which have extraordinary staying-power, have been detected almost everywhere, including in Arctic snow and the muscle-tissue of polar bears.

The river-route is one of the main ways by which muck gets into the sea, but it is not the only one. Although the dumping of high-level nuclear waste has largely been stopped, and the dumping of hazardous waste and sewage sludge is being stopped by degrees, dumping still goes on – legally and illegally. For one thing, so-called 'low-level' radioactive waste is still regularly discharged into the sea. For another, ships and other seagoing vessels push all kinds of rubbish overboard, including various forms of plastics which entangle marine life.

Also, medical waste is still sometimes disposed of in the sea – not the kind of substance you would choose to swim along with. And talking of substances you would not choose to swim with – enormous amounts of sewage are also discharged, raw and untreated, by several European countries, from pipes whose business-ends are often revealed at low tide.

Sewage is actually even more of a problem than it might appear. Strangely, though, it's hard to get the public – us – sufficiently worked up about it to complain much.

Most people, if confronted with a sinister, rusting metal canister nudging the shoreline, would quite rightly take dramatic action. They would

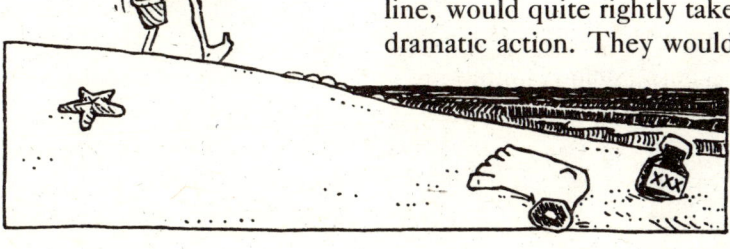

37

probably call the police – the local radio station – the nearest environmental pressure group – and generally make a big production about it until it was safely removed. They would also want to know if there were any more lurking in the deep.

The same people, though, faced with blobs of sewage in the seaweed and strips of sun-dried lavatory paper on the sand, simply avert their eyes and make discreet attempts to find a cleaner bit of beach.

The pressure group Surfers Against Sewage (whose name says it all) don't get as much media coverage for their demonstrations as they should. This seems to be because editors have decided that the huge inflatable turd which often accompanies them is in bad taste. It is not possible to explain why people find the protest itself in bad taste while – apparently – remaining unconcerned about the real and disgusting subject of the protest.

The sewage and the agricultural fertilisers share in the over-feeding of marine algae – and vast algae blooms, some species of which release toxins as part of their life-cycle, appear at sea as well as in rivers and streams. It's mainly a question of balance. The right amount of algae, in the right varieties, are an important oceanic food. If they grow so rapidly that they outstrip all predators they are a problem – partly when they die a natural death and turn slimy and revolting – and partly because the toxic sort seem to outstrip the non-toxic when over-nourished.

What is more, sewage is not the only thing that travels down sewers.

In Britain, the local Water

Authorities permit industries to disgorge a specified amount of toxic waste straight into the sewers. Some of these specified amounts are very high.

> "Information about discharges into the sewer network is a well-kept secret. The public has no legal right to see monitoring information – despite the fact that over 90% of industrial liquid waste is disposed of via this route." Friends of the Earth, 1993

Not all companies know exactly what chemicals they are discharging, or what the environmental effects are likely to be. Even when they do know what they are discharging – heavy metals, for example, in dangerous concentrations – they are within their rights to do so. (Heavy metals are used in various industrial processes, including the making of some plastics.)

If these heavy metals reach rivers and seas, they are often absorbed by fish or shellfish, which are then eaten by other animals, including humans.

When the seals off Britain died in droves a couple of years ago, as a result of a form of influenza, the polluters accepted no responsibility. It was an infection, they said, and not their fault. They were unwilling to consider the probability that, normally, the seals would have shaken off the infection – if their systems had not been thoroughly weakened by tainted water.

> "If I ruled the planet, every factory would have a water treatment plant and a smoke cleaner, public transport would be free, and there would be laws to ensure maximum security in transportation of oil and other dangerous materials, both by sea and by land." Lisa Friborg Møller, 17, Denmark

In the end, the human-created poison may actually poison a human – very rough justice indeed considering that the human who gets poisoned is extremely unlikely to be the one who caused the problem in the first place.

If the industrial pollution was kept separate from the sewage, all the human manure could be used as a fertiliser. As it is, it is too dangerous – and even when the sewage goes through the first treatment process, in which the solids are separated out, the resultant sewage sludge is often too toxic to use on the fields.

Probably the most famous polluter of the seas is oil – crude oil spilling from stricken tankers. Much more could be done to avoid these accidents. At the very least, it could be imperative for tankers to be built with double hulls. That way a sharp encounter with a rock wouldn't automatically result in an oil slick. But however horrified we may be at the damage caused by leaking oil, we can't claim to be totally innocent as long as we continue to want it – the energy it creates and the products that can be made from it.

Not all spillages are accidental. The oil released during the Gulf War was emptied out deliberately. So is the oil that is siphoned overboard when transport-ships swill out their tanks before taking in a new consignment.

> "Recently the Netherlands announced that it would not accept the discharge of Humber water from ships (which took it on as ballast when docked on the Humber) because it was too polluted." Greenpeace

Human manipulation of rivers and seas makes pollution worse. Some of the water from rivers which fed the land-locked Aral Sea in Russia has been diverted to irrigate cotton crops, which is why the sea is drying up and becoming ever saltier and less able to dilute impurities. It is now regarded as virtually dead.

Dam damage is another problem. The large-scale damming of rivers for irrigation, or to fill reservoirs, or to feed hydro-electric plants can have sad consequences. The eco-system below the dam suffers because its vital water supply is cut off, or cut down. The eco-system beside or above the dam may be flooded.

As well as ecological problems, there can be political problems too. Large rivers often flow across frontiers. What happens when one country creates a dam and lessens the flow to others? Drought? War?

Damming can also starve estuaries and deltas. The mighty Aswan dam has already changed the ecology of the once-rich Nile delta, and not for the better, either. More modest muddy estuaries, which may look flat and unappealing, support hugely varied forms of waterlife and wading birds. But only as long as the water flows.

Over-use of water is one of the most serious problems – and also the one that should be easiest to put right. Industrial processes can usually use recycled water – often their own recycled water – and domestic water-use in the rich countries could be cut by half, or more, without serious hardship. For a start, water companies could fix their leaking pipes.

Considering we are watery creatures living on a watery planet (more than 50% of our bodies are made of water and more than 70% of the surface of the planet is covered in it), it's really strange that we don't take it more seriously. And our lavish over-use of the stuff seems rather revolting when you think that in many Third World countries more than 50% of the population have no regular access to clean, safe water, nor any half-way hygenic sanitary arrangements.

> "If I ruled the planet I would make sure everyone knew ways of using water wisely. Water is our most important natural resource – without it no one could survive." Jaclyn Brown, 15, US

It isn't too late, but we're pushing our luck. Like mad magicians, we have taken

I WISH THESE KIDS WOULD CLEAN UP AFTER THEMSELVES

heavy metals, which were locked safely within the rocks, and released them to poison the earth, air and water. Like deranged alchemists, we have taken raw materials and not just shaped them into useful things, but changed them fundamentally, creating entirely new chemical compounds.

Or perhaps it isn't quite as dramatic as that. Perhaps we're more like arrogant chefs let loose in a large well-stocked kitchen – we've created wonderful and elaborate dishes, but we have no interest in clearing up after ourselves.

Industry has to clean up after itself, or at least pay for someone else to do it. Polluters, from the largest multinational company, to companies responsible for sewage works, to farmers, to the individuals who chuck horrors down domestic drains, have to take action.

There has been much political talk about making the polluter pay. This is fine. What is also necessary is detailed and regular monitoring of exactly what each one discharges, and in what form, and whether or not procedures could be adapted so that less is discharged in the first place.

Cleaning up is fine, but clean production – not creating the wastes at all – is even better.

> The Global Environment Monitoring System, sponsored by the UN, lists 158 heavily polluted rivers, among them the Ganges, Hudson, Loire, Mackenzie, Mekong, Mississippi, Missouri, Niger, Nile, Orinoco, Rhine, Thames, Volga, Yangtze and Zambesi.

Chapter Seven

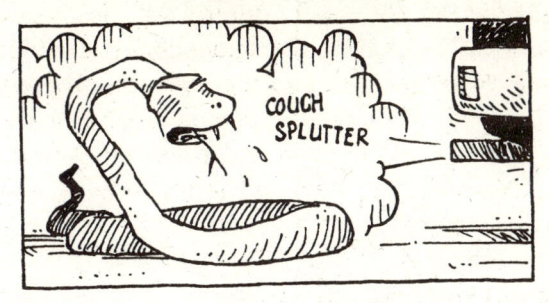

WHICH ARE THE MOST DANGEROUS POISONS?

There's no easy answer to that.

The venom of the sea snake, *hydrophis belcheri*, and the poison of the deathcap toadstool are both fatal in small doses. And you wouldn't want to meet a Brazilian wandering spider or a stonefish, either. On the other hand, these are all relatively rare and reasonably easy to avoid.

It takes a lot more carbon monoxide to have the same effect. But carbon monoxide has become quite common and a dose too small to kill is still enough to be less than healthy.

So it's hard to say which is the most dangerous.

In fact, except in extreme cases, it is exceedingly difficult to assess the exact risk factor of any chemical.

(The accident at Bhopal in India was an extreme case. People are still suffering severe after-effects, and still dying, ten years after the escape of the insecticide-ingredient methyl isocyanate from the Union Carbide plant. In Bhopal, the highly dangerous nature of the chemical was immediately, and cruelly, obvious.)

Millions of chemicals – many still undetected – occur naturally; they are the elements, substances and compounds of which all things are made. Thousands upon thousands have also been synthesised artificially for use in industry and elsewhere; and more are being developed daily.

Even the synthetic chemicals are not all fully identified. Sometimes it is simply not known how much of a specific synthetic chemical is in existence, or exactly how it achieves its intended effect.

An accurate assessment of the risk from chemical waste buried in a landfill site, for example, is only possible if an enormous amount of information can be collected. It would be necessary to know how much was buried and when, in what quantities it was leaking and how fast, whether it was polluting air, water or both. After that, it would be necessary to discover the extent of the area affected by the pollution, the quantity of polluted air or water being taken in by each individual in that area, and how often (twenty-four hours a day, only during working hours, or what). And then an assessment of the physical vulnerability of each of those individuals would be useful, and so it goes on.

This is why experts often seem to disagree – and why few are keen to give specific answers.

In fact, all chemicals are toxic – to a degree. Some are fatal in extremely small measures. Others are essential to biological life in the right amounts – indigestible if overdone – and only fatal in quantities so great that you probably wouldn't be able to get enough inside you to do any serious damage.

"All things are poisonous and nothing is poisonous. It is the dose which makes the poison." Paracelsus (real name Theophrastus Bombastus von Hohenheim), sixteenth-century alchemist.

Contrary to popular belief (Shock! Horror! Close down the Chemical Works!), some of the most potent poisons occur in nature.

> "The simple potato has about 100 different natural components ... some quite toxic ..." Joseph V. Rodricks, *Calculated Risks* (C.U.P., 1992)

Aflatoxin is a naturally toxic chemical, manufactured by a fungus. It can contaminate corn, peanuts and true nuts. You probably get a minimal dose in peanut butter, but would have to pig-out frequently and on a grand scale to do yourself damage.

Botulinum, found in soil, can be mega-toxic. If it finds its way into badly-preserved foods, it gives you botulism. This is frequently fatal – but mercifully extremely rare.

Other toxins which occur naturally aren't a problem unless used in a particular way – like tobacco plants. Tobacco smoke is one of the best-known, most extensively studied of all the toxins. Its negative effects on human health are understood very well. Some people, though, find self-inflicted risks acceptable and only get stroppy when they think about risks beyond their control – even if those risks aren't as high.

Then there are toxins which occur naturally but which only become a problem when gathered up and used in industrial processes – like heavy metals.

Heavy metals are mined, not made, and cannot be destroyed. They are used mainly in industrial and chemical processes, and released in the waste products into the earth, air and water, where they are major pollutants. The list of heavy metals currently contaminating the world is headed by arsenic, cadmium, lead, mercury and zinc.

Each of the heavy metals has numerous applications – these are a few:

Arsenic and its compounds (once the highly toxic star of a thousand early who-dunnits) is used in metal alloys, medicines and rat poison.

Cadmium goes into batteries and the rods for nuclear reactors. It is also the source of red, orange and yellow pigments for artists' colours and is one of the toxins drifting around in tobacco smoke. It can leach naturally out of

45

rocks and get into shellfish.

Lead is used in alloys (solder, for example), as sheeting to waterproof roofs and in shields for nuclear reactors. Now that the dangers of lead are understood it's no longer used for water-pipes, though old ones are still in use; it is present in compound form in 'leaded' petrol and some paints.

Mercury, found in thermometers, barometers and batteries, is used in the processing of gold, and the creation of chlorine. Chlorine, in turn, is used to bleach white paper, to sterilise and in the production of PVC plastics.

Zinc, which is a trace element, essential to life in appropriate amounts but a problem when there is overload, is used in metal alloys and pharmaceuticals; and in compound forms to preserve wood, as fireproofing and as a protective coating for metals (as in galvanizing).

Among the chemicals we have synthesised for our own purposes, toxicity is usually just an unfortunate side effect. Occasionally of course – as in the case of chemical warfare – it is the whole point. Not that we are the only creatures to use it.

> "In the chemical warfare arms race between plant and insect, the weaponry becomes enormously sophisticated. The neem tree uses azadirachtin in ways which – if a human developed it – would seem morally appalling: by suppressing insect appetites and stunting sexual development." Tim Redford, *The Guardian* (6 June 1992)

Organochlorine (otherwise known as chlorinated hydrocarbon) is the overall name for a group of synthetic chemical compounds. They have a variety of uses – with insecticides high on the list. They also feature in the manufacture of PVC (polyvinylchloride, non-biodegradable plastics used in packaging among other things), in solvents and in CFCs. They are created as a waste product when chlorine is used to bleach paper. They are highly toxic and they and their waste products hang around a long time.

> "Organochlorines are widely recognised as a group of highly toxic chemicals, causing a wide range of negative health effects in a broad array of species." Greenpeace

One of the organochlorines, PCB (polychlorinated biphenyl) originated as a by-product of the manufacture of some paints and electrical fittings. It is no longer in use but is still lurking in landfill sites. From here it can leach into underground water supplies, make its way to rivers and streams and contaminate fish.

> "If I ruled the planet I would ban all arms production and use the money saved to employ people to clean up polluted areas." Amandine Deguand, 17, France

When incinerated, organochlorines give off dioxins.

Dioxin (usually tetrachlorodibenzodioxin, one of a group of dioxins) is a highly poisonous gas, which first made the headlines as a side product of a defoliant used in Vietnam. It is one of several unpleasant PICs (Products of Incomplete

> **WANTED**
> PUBLIC ENEMY NUMBER 1
>
> DIOXIN
> ALIAS TETRACHLORODIBENZO-DIOXIN, MAY BE IN COMPANY OF PIC'S. USUALLY FOUND IN SMOKE
> DO NOT APPROACH
> **HIGHLY DANGEROUS**
> IF DISCOVERED, CONTACT AUTHORITIES

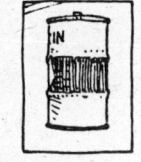

Combustion, if you'd prefer the full title). These are formed when toxic (and other) waste is incinerated. Even the apparently innocent garden bonfire can give off PICs, especially if someone chucks on odd bits of plastic or painted wood.

All large-scale industrial processes need electrical power, usually generated by the burning of fossil fuels, which give off sulphur dioxide, nitrogen oxides and hydrocarbons, sometimes with a dash of methane and non-methane volatile organic compounds thrown in.

Mineral oil (composed principally of hydrocarbons) may well also be a requirement for industry, since it is used as fuel and to make all the petroleum-based products, from petrol to plastics. Oil is a major pollutant when burned in any form – more so when spilled into the sea from tankers. Prince William Sound in Alaska may never fully recover from the 11 million gallons that poured out of the wrecked Exxon Valdez in 1989, and it will be a few years before the damage caused by the 85,000 tonnes lost by the Braer off the Shetlands in January 1993 can be fully assessed.

Nuclear power might be seen as a clean alternative to the burning of fossil fuels – but nuclear power is in decline. Though new nuclear power stations are currently being built, far more are being 'retired', much earlier than originally planned. It may be clean in action – but it is proving expensive and is haunted by more technical problems than expected. Also it is unpopular – more so since the disaster in 1986 at the nuclear plant in Chernobyl, where decontamination work continues.

Even if accidents could somehow be prevented, there will always be the grim problem of nuclear waste. Waste management techniques are inadequate and also nuclear waste remains potent for thousands of years.

> "No scientist or engineer can give an absolute guarantee that radioactive waste will not someday leak in dangerous quantities from even the best of repositories." Konrad Krauskopf, Stanford University Geologist, *Science* (1990)

To return to the industrial processes – once the products have been made, they have to be transported. If they go by road, the exhausts of the vehicles which carry them give out more sulphur dioxide and nitrogen oxides, with a generous helping of carbon monoxide.

All these fumes, from factory or truck, contribute to the greenhouse effect, to acid rain and to choking surface ozone. The trucks (in common with private cars and petrol refineries) also give out benzene (C_6H_6), a carcinogenic (cancer-causing) hydrocarbon (sometimes used as an industrial solvent).

So many dangers to choose from – which would you pick and how would you choose?

In the end, although the question 'which is the most dangerous?' is often asked, it isn't really possible to answer it, or even particularly useful to try. What is more important is to understand that chemistry is usually complex – and that it is not possible or practical to stop all these processes and instantly get rid of any compound that can be seen to do any damage.

> "If I ruled the planet, I would shut down all the factories and power stations to stop pollution."

A questionnaire, sent by the publishers of this book to teenagers in several European countries, the US and Canada, drew this answer from several teenagers in each country.

If you agree with this, then are you willing to do without the things power stations and factories provide? Are you really willing to do without light and heat, and almost every mass-produced consumer product? There goes the computer, the TV, the camera, the car, the boots, the bus, the burger, the walkman, the paint on the walls and the pill to cure your splitting headache.

What is more relevant is to think about over-population – the more people there are, the more they will use. And about over-consumption – most people in the developed countries use considerably more than their fair share of just about everything. And about clean production, which means cutting down on toxic by-products and waste. And about proper funding for research so that the technology which inadvertently created a lot of the problems can be adapted to solve them.

As we've known for a long time now, the most dangerous thing on the planet is not dioxin, not the Australian sea-wasp jellyfish, not sulphur dioxide, or mercury, or botulism – but humankind, the greedy apes.

> Carbon Monoxide, CO, occurs naturally; is present in car exhausts and cigarette smoke; is given off in relatively small amounts (together with large amounts of carbon dioxide) when fossil fuels are burned; is manufactured by the chemicals industry as part of the plastics and paint making processes (among other things). Can't be seen or smelt, but kills by combining with haemoglobin in blood, preventing it from carrying oxygen round the body.

DANGEROUSNESS OLYMPICS

Chapter Eight

WHAT ARE WE DOING TO OTHER SPECIES?

Not much that's nice.

An Army Research Laboratory in America has apparently found that it is possible to sticky-tape golden orb-web spiders flat on their backs so that a minute spindle can draw out their silk, which is then used to make bullet-proof vests. It is reported that each spider can be stuck to the production line again and again. It is not reported what eventually happens to the empties – although it seems unlikely that anyone has set up a sanctuary for clapped-out crawlies.

If time travel and interspecies communication ever become a possibility, then someone should go back far enough to warn animals not to trust humans, to say: "It starts out all right. You get to shelter in our caves and sit by our fires and gnaw on left-over deer bones. But the next thing you

51

know we're forcing you to smoke and dripping shampoo in your eyes to see if you go blind."

It isn't clear exactly when we decided we had the right to regard animals either as irrelevant (let's chop down the rainforest, who cares what lives there) or designed entirely to serve us (quick, peel me an Ecuadorian frog, there's a chemical painkiller in the skin which is even stronger than morphine).

It's true that all the great Creation Myths suggest that we are in some way superior to other species, and, indeed, that they have been put into our charge. However, it isn't obligatory to exploit whatever you're in charge of – traditional, maybe, but obligatory, no.

It isn't all our fault.

We have to eat, so from the beginning we were obliged to hunt for other life forms – animal and vegetable – in order to be able to do this. Later we realised it was much more convenient to plant the fruit and vegetables near to hand and to fence some of the animals in so they could be caught more easily. If not pushed too far, this system did little damage.

The trouble is we always do push things too far.

First, we prospered and multiplied. This gave us the leisure to discover greed and the sheer weight of numbers to develop arrogance. For a long time we have understood the natural laws that say that everything must adjust to its changing environment or die. Unfortunately, until very recently, we have always refused to accept that these laws apply to us. We are The Lords of the Earth – the environment must adapt to us.

Instead of keeping a pig and some chickens in the garden and a few cattle in a field nearby, we decided we'd get far more meat if we crammed a lot of animals into tiny spaces, indoors, in conditions you would think would be too horrible to contemplate, let alone create on purpose.

Even when we discovered we didn't have to eat meat every day (or, indeed, at all) in order to survive, we refused to adapt. The majority of us in the rich countries continued to demand meat at every main meal, even though new methods of storing and transporting food meant we could get hold of pretty much anything else we wanted, including beans, pulses, nuts and other sources of protein, and despite the fact that an excess of beef cattle is environmentally damaging.

In the early days of hunting for food, animal skins were needed to make clothes and shelters. Even though this is no longer true, many of us still want the skins. We have somehow formed the idea that they look as beautiful on us as they did on their original owners – and, naturally, the rarer the animal the more valued is its fur.

The fur trade claims that it's acceptable to kill animals for their skins if they've been bred on a ranch for that express purpose. But is that true? Is it acceptable to keep mink without any access to water, even though their partly-webbed feet make it moderately obvious that they are semi-aquatic? Is it acceptable to keep an arctic fox, which would normally range around quite a large personal territory, in a small wire cage? Or to separate cubs from their mother and from each other in case they damage their pelts while they're playing? These skins have to be absolutely perfect – fur-farm customers are picky people, they're not like Davy Crockett who'd wear anything. (This introduces another pro-fur-farm argument, which says that if the animals were stressed or unhealthy their coats would be tatty and useless. If you feel that fur-farming is **not** acceptable, be warned that you will have to develop a very strong case if you hope to win a debate with a mink rancher.)

As well as eating and wearing other species, we decided we'd like to share our lives with them.

Now the average potted ivy or domestic cat does rather well out of this arrangement. (In fact, most plants and animals, even those which were originally exotic, may survive quite cheerfully if bred in the country where they are to be kept.) Also, the owners of well-kept pets, or 'companion animals' as some people prefer to call them, tend to be more aware of other species and of their needs than the pet-less among the population. It's one of the few areas where friendly inter-species communication – admittedly at a fairly simple level – is possible.

> Cats are carnivores – don't try to turn them into vegetarians!

Unfortunately the high prices paid for rare and exotic plants tempt collectors to risk wiping out whole species by pillaging the wilderness for them. And the desire to own interesting pets leads to the capture of, for example, thousands of parrots, many of which will be crushed or suffocated to death on the tortuous journey from forest to pet shop, and few of which are likely to be entirely happy, even in the best of homes, living in exile with a chain round one ankle. (Happily, tortoises are now spared the experience of being stacked on top of each other in crates and shipped to British pet stores. It is now illegal to sell a tortoise in this country unless you can prove it was bred over here.)

WHO'S A PRETTY BOY THEN?

WE WERE

Next, we decided to use other species for medical experiments. This is a complicated issue. It is impossible to defend the use of animals to test cosmetics. However, it is not easy to explain to the mother of a child suffering from leukaemia that you don't think that a laboratory-bred animal should be sacrificed, even if its death might lead to her child's cure.

Animals are also used to test the degree of toxicity of certain chemicals. When deciding whether or not laboratory animals should be used in this way, it's only fair also to consider the health of people who have to work with dangerous industrial compounds. And before deciding that no one should have to go anywhere near the stuff, it's relevant to consider whether or not you are willing to do without the end-products.

What is certain is that vivisection as a teaching aid is almost never (if ever) justifiable. Killing animals first and then dissecting them is also going out of fashion. Even if it is decided that laboratory tests are necessary, pain and distress should obviously be kept to a minimum.

There are increasing numbers of doctors and nurses in several countries, including Britain, who believe that no animal experiments are appropriate. They maintain that, apart from anything else, animal and human physiologies are so different that the results can actually be misleading.

These 'Doctors and Nurses Against Animal Experiments' point out that all the drugs in recent years which have been found, too late, to have unacceptable side effects had been thoroughly tested on animals, and that these tests had not shown up the problems.

Thalidomide, for example, which was prescribed for pregnancy-nausea and which turned out to be capable of causing birth defects, had been fully tested on animals. So had the anti-arthritic drug Opren, whose unacceptable side effects included death.

Others are equally convinced that some animal testing is an essential part of the development of medicines to control disease and pain – and not only in human animals but also in domestic, farm and even wild animals as well.

And yet, perversely, even though it is widely agreed that the rainforests, and the other wild places of the world, contain all manner of medicinal plants which would be of huge benefit to us, we haven't yet quite found an effective way of protecting them.

Of all the things we do to other species, there is one which rushes them towards the brink of extinction faster than the rest. It isn't killing for fun (the way the French sailors wiped out the dodo), or hunting and trapping for the sake of fur and horn, nor even the international trade in exotic plants and animals, though they all play their part.

> "... it's easy to think that as a result of the extinction of the dodo we are now sadder and wiser, but there's a lot of evidence to suggest we are merely sadder and better informed." Douglas Adams, *Last Chance to See* (Pan Books 1991)

The greatest danger of all is not direct attack, but simply a side-effect of entirely different activities – the widespread destruction of habitats.

For more details on this destruction, see almost any of the other chapters. It is achieved in many ways, including by cutting down the rainforests, by polluting the earth and water, by creating environmental disasters such as wars, oil-spills, or nuclear accidents, by draining or polluting wetlands, by cutting peat from bogs, by climate-change caused by the greenhouse effect, by the destruction wrought by acid rain, by the increased ultraviolet radiation admitted by the thinning ozone layer, by the use of artificial fertilisers and pesticides . . .

Even so, not all extinction is the fault of the human species.

We didn't invent the phenomenon. Extinction is part of the natural rhythm of life on this planet and was going on long before we evolved.

What we *are* responsible for is speeding up the process. Since we don't even know how many species (plant and animal) exist on earth at the present moment, let alone how many existed at any given time in the past, all figures have to be arrived at by educated guesswork.

Greenpeace estimates the natural rate of extinction at one species every hundred years, and the accelerated rate caused specifically by human behaviour at one species every thirty minutes. No one can prove or disprove this estimate, but even if things are not as bad as all that, there is no doubt that the rate of extinction is speeding up and that we are the cause of it.

> *"We ought to be putting more effort into having a go at predicting what's on Earth now, because the stars will still be there for astronomers to study in 100 years time, whereas patterns of biological diversity will have gone by then. Ours is a time-limited science: we are not going to be able to do much of it in 100 years."*
> Professor John Lawton, who runs the National Environment Research Council's population biology unit at Silwood Park, interviewed in The Guardian *(5 June 1992)*

In all this, it's important to

remember that not only do the rich countries do most of the damage, they extend the damage into poorer countries and then, not infrequently, try to push much of the blame on to them as well.

"It is difficult for a man scavenging on the garbage dump created by affluence and profligate consumption to understand that protecting a bird is more important than protecting him." Anwar Saifullah Khan of Pakistan speaking to The Guardian *(6 June 1992)*

If we value other species – not just because they might be beneficial to us in some way, but for their own sake, out of respect for the fascinating intricacy of the film of life on the surface of the Earth – we have to change our behaviour.

We have the ability to destroy the whole lot, including ourselves. We have the power. We have the technology.

We also have the ability, the power and the technology to save them. It would be nice if we used it.

> *Skins:* Japan is the top legal importer of cat skins (34,696); the US is the top legal importer of reptile skins (1,641,308), with Japan second (950,047) and France third (883,971). *Live Animals:* The US is the top legal importer of parrots (277,432) and of primates (13,811), with Japan second top importer of primates (7,133) and the UK third both of primates (5,717) and of parrots (40,771). Legally imported live animals may travel in reasonable conditions, but an estimated 60% of smuggled animals die in transit. Figures assessed in the late 1980s by CITES.

Chapter Nine

END-OF-TERM REPORTS ON INDUSTRIAL COUNTRIES

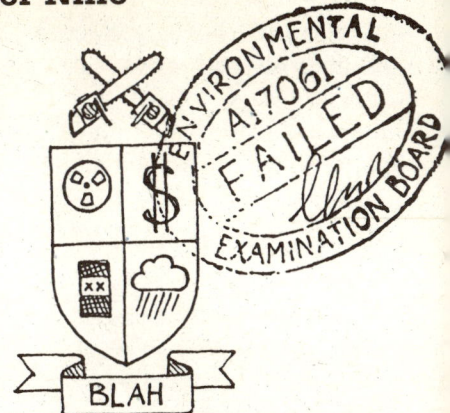

Or: Could do better.

If the industrial revolution had never happened, we wouldn't be in this mess. We'd be in an entirely different mess.

However, now we're in this one, we can't back off. The only way out of it is through it. The industrial countries, in particular, have to try to find ways of using science and technology to cure the problems they've created.

It isn't easy to offer a detailed end-of-term report on every country on the face of the planet. For one thing, there is more information available on some than on others. For another thing, term doesn't end, it goes on, policies change, and yesterday's polluter may be today's honourable green.

This is how it looks in a few selected countries at the moment.

General report on the European Union

It doesn't make sense to deal with the EU as a whole because the individual member countries still operate different policies in certain areas.

A quick alphabetical glance through some of them suggests the following:

59

Britain, at the moment, appears to have collected nothing but bad marks.

It imports more tropical timber (legally and illegally) and empties more heavy metal wastes into the seas than anyone else in the EU.

> *"Three-quarters of the sewage from Britain's coastal towns and cities is discharged raw, without even minimal treatment ... More than a quarter of Britain's beaches regularly fail European Commission safety standards."*
> G Lean and D Hinrichsen The World Wildlife Fund Atlas of the Environment *(Helicon Publishing Ltd, 1992)*

A significant percentage of its drinking water contains more nitrates (seeping into water systems from fertilisers) than EU guidelines permit.

Despite its stated concern about tropical rainforests, it seems barely capable of protecting its own ancient woodland from destruction in favour of new roads or plantations of swift-growing, commercially useful Sitka Spruce which offer extremely limited wildlife habitation.

Its attitude to waste – especially for such a small country – is extraordinary. It buries almost all of it, toxic or domestic, and largely untreated. There are believed to be well over 4,000 dumps of which 1,300 are a threat to underground freshwater sources. (Friends of the Earth say these 1,300 have been known about for roughly twenty years.)

It is trying to cut domestic energy use and is beginning to get serious about wind power. Nevertheless, 'could do better'.

Denmark is looking good. A generous scattering of wind turbines produces 2% of its total electricity; its recycling record is impressive (it has outlawed many non-refillable drinks containers, including cans); its toxic waste disposal systems should become a model for other countries. Waste is collected, sorted, treated, and buried only when safe. The portion of it which is burned fuels the central heating of half the houses near the disposal plant at Nyborg.

France already has one plant to harness tide-power, more than a thousand hydropower plants, and is planning a major investment in electric taxis in 10 of its cities.

On the negative side, it admits to well over 400 neglected toxic waste dumps, 80 of them in a particularly dangerous condition.

It is far more open to the idea of organic farming than some countries, but must take some responsibility for the 200 million Asian bullfrogs killed every year so their hindlegs can be fried in garlic. India has banned their export because of public outcry about the way the frogs are killed (the relevant bits cut off and frozen and the rest left to die, neither quickly nor peacefully).

> *"Malaria is on the upsurge in Asia because of over-harvesting of bullfrogs which eat the mosquitoes that carry the disease."* CITES (Convention on International Trade in Endangered Species of Wild Flora and Fauna), G Lean and D Hinrichsen The World Wildlife Fund Atlas of the Environment *(Helicon Publishing Ltd, 1992)*

France is also third in the league of legal importers of reptile skins.

Germany has a mixed record. The old East Germany is over-burdened with toxic waste – but to be fair, much of it was exported there from the West. The old West Germany admits to approximately 15,000 dumps full of hazardous waste that should be dealt with as soon as possible.

In its favour, it can be said that Germany is a world-leader in rubbish-reduction and packaging-limitation; is as serious about reusable drinks containers as Denmark; has 3,000 small hydro-power plants, is planning several wind farms and is researching into other renewable energy technologies; and is effective about reducing the industrial use of water (and of recycling what is used). It is also a major manufacturer of equipment for improving the industrial environment.

> *"State of the art paper manufacturing plants there now use only 7 kilograms of water to produce a kilogram of paper, 1 per cent as much as older factories elsewhere."* State of the World *Worldwatch Institute Report, (Earthscan 1993)*

On the negative side, ships regularly leave the country

carrying toxic waste because German industrialists maintain they have 'no more room for it at home'. In Albania in 1993 it was discovered that people had been spreading German toxic waste on their crops under the impression that 'chemicals from the West are good fertilisers'. And all Germany's major rivers are severely polluted.

The Netherlands, famous for its windmills and suitably flat and windy, is planning major wind farm projects. It is spending large sums on clearing up the dumping grounds where toxic and other hazardous wastes are in a dangerous state. (You could say it's a shame the waste was so badly dealt with in the first place in so many countries, but at least some seem to be taking action, at last.)

It is also using the power of money extremely effectively – environmental taxes and grants mean that companies who pollute lose out financially, while those who clean up, gain.

Norway's strongest subject is the sea – with mixed results. It created the first ever wave-power plant (altogether, roughly half the energy the country uses comes from wave, wind or solar power). On the other hand, together with Iceland, it has taken up commercial whaling once more.

Spain isn't the best country at anything in particular – but then it isn't the worst, either. It's very good at keeping its beaches clean and is planning windfarm projects. (Also it bans the use of cars in Madrid when air pollution levels reach dangerous highs – which sounds good until you realise how appalling it is that pollution should ever reach such a pitch.)

On the other hand, over-use of water has severely damaged the important Doñana Wetlands, and towards the end of 1992 an article in *New Scientist* claimed that 'millions of animals, including endangered species such as lynx, wolf and several species of vulture, die each year on Spanish roads.' Chameleons seem to be the worst hit, literally – Spanish drivers have been seen to swerve over them deliberately.

Sweden is a star when it comes to pollution limitation. A somewhat complex system of permits controls industrial waste and compels the companies responsible to process it before discharging it. It also treats almost 100% of its sewage and is using compressed natural gas for much of its urban public transport.

General report on Australia
Australia has the greatest of all coral reefs – the 1,200 mile-long Great Barrier Reef – which is generally regarded as being in good shape and 'well managed'. In common with other reefs, it is beginning to suffer from too much ultraviolet radiation (due to the thinning ozone layer) but the Australian Institute of Marine Sciences has recently synthesised a chemical which helps protect coral from sunburn. One of the leading bodies researching into the effects of ultraviolet radiation on crops, The Commonwealth Scientific and Industrial Research Organisation, is here, too. Also on the plus side, Australia has a good record on urban water conservation. You would expect it to be making reasonable use of renewable energy resources (wave, geothermal, wind and solar power), and it is. Although Sydney suffers severe air pollution, there isn't much trouble from acid rain.

On the minus side, the river system is being polluted by agro-chemicals and domestic waste, and although there is genuine concern for conservation, the temperate rainforests of Tasmania are heavily logged. More marks are lost on the subject of soil erosion. Australians are dedicated meat-eaters (second only to North Americans) and have allowed their cattle and sheep (not to mention horses and rabbits) to overgraze to such an extent – without taking any measures to protect the land – that the topsoil is blowing away at an alarming rate, expecially serious in a country with so much natural desert.

General report on Canada
Canada, with its forests, its water, its vast spaces, should be – could be – one of the most truly environmentally

friendly countries to be found anywhere.

But it isn't.

In Canada's defence it has to be said that most of its bad marks have been awarded by its own government, in a report released in the spring of 1992.

Canada has confessed to destroying vast swathes of forest; to contaminating the Great Lakes with as many as 300 chemical pollutants; to allowing over 1,400 smaller lakes to become clear and lifeless as a result of acid rain; to turning many of its freshwater supplies into a health hazard; to eroding the prairies with intensive agriculture; to playing a significant part in thinning the ozone layer; and to achieving third place in the list of carbon dioxide manufacturers.

In common with the people of most countries, Canadians seem to have over-estimated their fair share of the Earth's resources. The *New Scientist* reports that Bill Rees of the University of British Columbia has calculated that the maintenance of every single Canadian, at current levels of consumption, would take 3 hectares of ecosystem. He says, "If you multiply that by the population of the world, you'd need two and a half Earths to support the present world population."

Admitting its mistakes, Canada has produced a Green Plan. It'd be unfair to judge too harshly until it has had time to put this into practice.

General report on Japan

Japan is top in energy efficiency, and should be an example to the rest of the world. It is also ahead in renewable-energy technology and has an impressive record in industrial water-economy, recycling much of the water used by the iron and steel and paper-making industries. In fact, Japan earns gold stars for recycling generally, and for dealing with domestic waste so efficiently that less than a fifth goes into landfill sites.

"Japan, the largest industrial world-producer [of bicycles] has an [annual] output of just under 8 million. In contrast to the US, where most bicycles are used by children or recreational riders, bikes in Japan are widely used for commuting." Marcia D. Lowe, quoting from Interbike Directory,

in Vital Signs *(Earthscan, 1992-93)*

Furthermore, at the Rio Summit, Japan was particularly attentive and keen to contribute.

The bad marks start when Japan's attitude to Third World countries is examined. It stands accused of using its aid budget to manipulate developing countries, and its record on rainforest depletion is bad. And the world's wildlife would be unlikely to rate Japan as favourite nation. Its enormously high level of fishing – highest of any country in the world – is totally unsustainable. It is heavily into whaling. Its decision to turn its tidal flats into docks and marinas has had a discouraging effect on the many migratory birds who used to stopover there.

Finally, it is almost certainly the largest commercial receiver of illegally acquired wildlife, alive, dead or skinned. (Illegal trade is always easier when a country has a flourishing legal trade.)

General report on New Zealand

Most of the time, New Zealand is well-behaved. As one of the member states of the IUCN, the World Conservation Union, it is concerned to protect its natural habitats and its three major national parks cover lowland areas as well as the more scenic and dramatic mountainous ones. It is not into whaling, and although it is among the top fishing nations of the world it doesn't seem to be taking too much. The geological structure of the area means that there are major deposits of hot water trapped in the underlying rock – in other words, geothermal power is available and New Zealand is making good use of it. It employs other forms of renewable energy as well (hydroelectric, solar and wind), 80% of its taxis and buses run on compressed natural gas, and, not surprisingly, its air quality is good.

Nobody's perfect, though, and New Zealand does suffer significant coastal pollution. Furthermore, not only is it enthusiastic about fertilisers and pesticides, its agricultural methods are causing soil degradation, including loss of topsoil. Also, although by world standards it is a relatively low producer of toxic waste, it has an unfortunate tendency to dump what it does produce in a deep-sea offshore site.

General report on Russia

No ecological report on Russia can be anything but seriously depressing. Almost the single good thing that can be said is that it is co-operating with the US on nuclear arms reduction.

The former Soviet Union ranks second only to the US in its contribution to the greenhouse effect. Russia itself produces 70% of what was the Soviet Union's toxic waste – most of it dumped untreated in unsuitable sites (though it cannot compete with the US for casual abandonment of hazardous material). Its radioactive waste is dealt with in much the same way.

Possibly as much as half its fresh water is contaminated, and a significant portion of its food. The land-locked Aral Sea is virtually lifeless. Radiation sickness (fortunately in a small minority) is a reality. Life expectancy is dropping.

"We have already doomed ourselves for the next 25 years. The new generation is entering adult life unhealthy." Vladimir Pokrovsky, Russian Academy of Medical Sciences, quoted in State of the World *(Earthscan, 1993)*

At least, like Canada in its different way, Russia admits to the problems – and this may make change possible.

General report on the US

This country has achieved top marks for soil erosion control (the rest of the world should pay attention to its methods) and for steel recycling (which saves energy and cuts both pollution and the use of water). Together with the late USSR – and now with Russia which still has control of most Eastern bloc nuclear weapons – it seems to be making an honest attempt to cut the nuclear threat.

"The stage is set for a dramatic decrease in the world's nuclear arsenal. But it will still contain enough firepower to annihilate life on earth, and none of the nuclear powers is publicly contemplating the eventual abolition of nuclear weapons." Michael Renner, Vital Signs, *Worldwatch Institute Report (Earthscan, 1992-93)*

The US has also impressed the examiners with its attention to water-use. Several industries have found a variety of ways of using less. Fourteen states have already decreed that new showerheads, taps and toilets must be more water-efficient, and other states are likely to follow.

California, in particular, gets additional marks for its steadily increasing production of solar and wind power, its 'zero-emissions' policy and its growing use of electric cars. (It should be aware, though, of the argument that says that though electric cars create less pollution on the streets, they are responsible for more at the power station and factory.)

Unfortunately, the US is a world leader in other, less appealing, ways. It is the chief contributor to the greenhouse effect. It comes first in the 'abandoned-toxic-waste-dumps' class (estimates of the number of dangerous sites, needing urgent attention, vary between 2,500 and 10,000).

And its energy efficiency leaves a great deal to be desired.

California drops marks for the density and severity of air pollution in the whole Los Angeles basin; for the chemical pollution which has caused the deaths of waterbirds in the Kesterson National Wildlife Refuge; and for the abuse and misuse of water which has put Mono Lake, near Yosemite, at risk.

In fact, all this water-saving is not before time. The US in general has already lost half its wetlands, with all their rich diversity of life, and drained and degraded the Everglades to such an extent that the State of Florida has been shocked into launching a ten-year save-the-swamps campaign.

What is more – rainforests aren't the only forests in the world which suffer – deforestation in North America has had a predictably bad effect on bird life, with severe loss of numbers and possible loss of species.

The US disgraced itself at the Rio Summit in 1992 by refusing to sign the Climate Change Convention and the Biodiversity Agreement, but President Clinton will sign both, though in a watered-down form. (President Clinton seems to want to be environmentally friendly – but will the powerful US industrialists permit this?)

If these countries really were college students preparing for exams, the most striking thing about their situation would be this: the date of the finals is not known. Speedy revision would seem to be essential – and, in the circumstances, no one should hesitate to share or copy each other's good ideas.

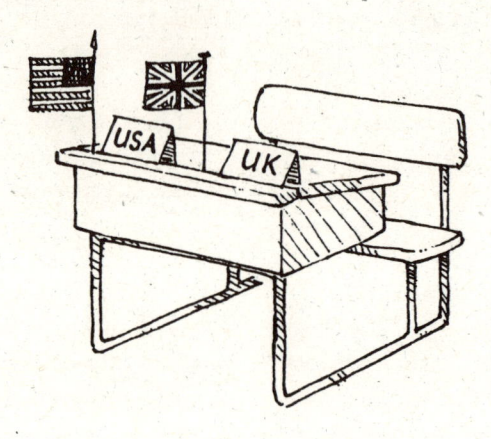

Chapter Ten

AND NOW FOR THE GOOD NEWS...

Or: Don't give up yet, just as it's beginning to come right...

If you're not worried about the state of the planet, that's really surprising.

If you are worried, it would be a mistake to react with panic and depression – however logical those reactions might seem in weak moments.

You can only do what you can do (which might, in fact, be quite a lot). But it's cheering to know that there are enormous numbers of other people who are also doing what they can do.

In Britain alone there are more than 7,500 environmental organisations, many of them international. Worldwide, there are many thousands more. In almost every country in the First World, Second World and Third World people are working on behalf of common sense and a sustainable future. Here are just some of the recent achievements, large or small, of those who would quite like things to get better, fast.

Damning the dams
In 1989 a coalition of groups saved a huge tract of Amazonian rainforest which the Brazilian state electricity company planned to flood for a series of hydro-electric dams. Friends of the Earth helped co-ordinate local pro-

test and presented it not just to the Brazilian Government but also to the international banks who were putting up the money. With world public opinion against them, they backed off.

The last wild place?
In 1991 it was finally agreed that the Antarctic should be preserved as wilderness for at least fifty years. This was a huge victory for Greenpeace who had to persuade the Antarctic Treaty Nations to give up all thoughts of extracting the valuable minerals known to lie hidden there.

Watch your step
Local governments in Japan have found a way of recycling waste sewage-sludge into paving slabs.

> "In 1990, after concerted international campaigning by Greenpeace, the North Sea Ministers Conference agreed to a wide range of policy measures to clean up the North Sea. The UK, although lagging far behind other European countries, again under pressure from Greenpeace, agreed end dates for UK sewage sludge dumping in the North sea (1998) and industrial waste dumping (1993)."
> Greenpeace pamphlet, (April 1992)

Green prizes
In Britain in 1993 the new Queen's Award to Industry for Environmental Achievement came into being. Products have to be practical and commercially viable as well as specifically environmentally friendly (though obviously every product has some environmental impact).

High-powered washing
Research in the US and Britain, though still in its early stages, suggests that within ten years it may well be possible to dispose of many forms of toxic waste by means of

chemical reactions made possible when high temperatures and high pressure raise ordinary water to a 'supercritical' state.

ECO-ice
A German company, DKK, is marketing a CFC-free fridge known as Greenfreeze, which functions on small amounts of propane and butane gas (ie no CFCs) and which will be available by the time this book is published. At least two other fridge manufacturers are following suit.

This, that and the otter
The UN and the EU have both banned drift-netting – all that remains now is for the ban to be enforced in all places.

Shire horses are making a come-back for use on farms. David Fitch of Chestnut Tree Farm, West Sussex, retiring after breeding them for forty years, told *The Independent*:

"They have always provided the cheapest form of transport for deliveries within three miles of a base."

Otters are returning to the River Severn after an absence of over thirty years.

Gleam of hope
Low energy light bulbs are now widely available. They seem expensive, but because their use reduces electricity bills they should pay for themselves within six months (they last a lot longer than that).

Safe sea air
In 1988 the efforts of Greenpeace led to a global ban on the burning of toxic waste at sea.

Algae power
At the University of the West of England in Bristol, a system has been developed to use solar power to grow chlorella, a form of algae. The algae is then dried and burned to generate electricity. The carbon dioxide released by the burning process is fed to the next generation of algae, which use it for photosynthesis. A satisfyingly closed system!

Factory-farmed tomatoes?
Research at the University of Strathclyde has come up with a way of diverting the carbon dioxide from factory emissions into a greenhouse to help sustain its tomato plants. The greenhouse has to be very near the factory, and means must be found of removing toxins from the fumes, but this is clearly a potential success.

Support for farmers
The British government is making grants to farmers whose land lies in environmentally sensitive areas (ESAs) so they can cut back on potentially destructive intensive farming without losing income. And the largest private landowner in England and Wales, the National Trust, has agreed to accept lower rent for a while from any tenant farmer who wants to convert to 'organic' farming.

From petroleum to plastic to petrol
In Japan, Toshiba are working on a method of transforming chloride-based plastics back into fuel oil and petrol.

Old cars for new
The government of the Netherlands is levying a tax on new cars which will pay for the recycling of old ones, while in Britain BMW and a scrap merchant have joined forces to form a vehicle recycling plant.

> "Between 1988, the peak year of production, and 1991, world production of chlorofluorocarbons fell by an astounding 46 per cent." State of the World, *Worldwatch Institute Report (Earthscan, 1993)*

Kew goes green

When confronted with infestations of mealy-bugs, the glasshouse-gardeners at the Royal Botanic Gardens in Kew no longer respond with blasts of pesticide – since 1992 they have used lizards and predatory ladybirds instead. Also, both Kew and the Botanical Gardens in New York have a requirement that companies agree to pay royalties to developing countries before commercial research is undertaken on their plants.

A load of airwash

Pay attention, this one's peculiar. A company in the States has developed a machine with a generator which uses an electrical discharge to split the oxygen molecules found in ordinary air. Some of the wandering atoms recombine as ozone. Dirty laundry is put into this machine and when it is taken out again it is clean. The machine works fast, uses very little energy, only a minimal amount of water (as a coolant) and no detergent. It can't cope with fat or grease, but since it's now in use in several hotels and prisons it must be good with dust, dandruff and general grime.

Dung Ho!

While questing through horse dung in pursuit of beneficial bacteria, John Pirt of King's College, London, has discovered one that breaks down the solids in sewage. A prototype system will soon be available for testing.

Shredding the bedding

Increasingly, old telephone directories and newspapers

are being shredded and used as bedding material for cattle, horses and other domestic animals. It's more comfortable than sawdust or straw, flies don't lay eggs in it, bacteria don't breed in it, and when it's dirty it makes great fertiliser mulch. (There have been no recorded cases of calves phoning home.)

Seeing the wood *and* the trees
In the summer of 1993, after years of campaigning, environmentalists and local protesters won a hugely important victory in Britain. They succeeded in forcing the government to abandon plans to destroy part of the ancient and valuable Oxleas Wood by running a major road through it. (The road was to have linked up with the proposed East London River Crossing, ELRIC, over the Thames at Woolwich.)

A future for the forests
Several countries, including India and the Philippines, are taking serious steps to protect their rainforests, and local environmental groups in India, Indonesia, Columbia and Kenya, among other countries, are organising major and very successful tree-planting campaigns.

No more hedgehog-six-packs
The complaints from Saint Tiggywinkles Wildlife Hospital, which often has to rescue animals trapped in the hoops of the plastic carriers discarded from six-packs, have at last been attended to by the manufacturers. ITW Hi-cone have developed a new type which becomes brittle and crumbles away within six weeks.

Planet power
In 1993 The Worldwatch Institute reported steady growth in the generation of wind-power and geothermal power.

'Peat partnership'

Under pressure from Friends of the Earth, most British garden centres have acknowledged that peat cutting does damage and are now offering alternatives to peat-based potting composts. They carry signs to show they've entered into the 'Peat Partnership'.

And finally . . .

Agenda 21 is coming to a town near you

It is fairly widely known that the Earth Summit at Rio de Janeiro in 1992 produced a set of environmental commitments which are now to be reassessed and recommitted annually. The overall title is Agenda 21 (for 21st century). What is slightly less widely known, for some reason, is this: it was also agreed that, within the next three years, all the local governments within the signing countries must produce individual Agenda 21s, in consultation with local people concerned with their own immediate environments.

This could turn out to be the most effective mechanism yet for enabling voters to push governments, both local and national, in the right direction. Don't waste it. Sort out your ideas in good time, and if you don't have a vote, start working on those around you who do.

Chapter Eleven

GET CLEAN

Or: If I smell, blame the environment.

When you leave the bathroom, by the door, do you ever think what else is leaving at the same time, through the waste pipes?

The answer depends on what you were doing in there, but the potential list is long – lavatory paper, sewage, sanitary protection, toothpaste, shampoo, yesterday's styling mousse, conditioner, shaving cream (and bristles), soap, bath oil, (and the various assorted detergents, dyes and perfumes in those products), approximately 40 litres of water (more than double that if you had a bath instead of a shower, and even more if you left the tap running while you scrubbed your teeth) and, if you cleaned up after yourself, bleach, bath cleaner and limescale remover. Also a dose of that stuff that turns the water blue – or green! – with every flush, and probably contains as many pollutants as it's supposed to get rid of.

Not everything in this grotesque cocktail is harmful, but the local sewage works still has to deal with it (or not, as the case may be), and the local reservoir has to supply all the water you chose to use.

> THE BIGGEST WASTE OF WATER IN THE COUNTRY BY FAR IS WHEN YOU SPEND HALF A PINT AND FLUSH TWO GALLONS *

* HRH THE DUKE OF EDINBURGH

A thought: what if you were going on a trip, somewhere good, somewhere you really wanted to go, and you were told you had to get everything you needed into a backpack? It's unlikely you'd attempt to take your share of the bathroom – more likely you'd pick out a basic kit. So if that'll do when you're out having a good time, why do you need so much more when you're staying home?

Few bodies are so filthy that they couldn't be cleaned quite satisfactorily with a small amount of water and a few swipes of colourless unscented soap. And a toothbrush would be handy and some unbleached lavatory paper.

It isn't necessary to be quite that spartan – but if you manage to convince yourself that those few things are all that's necessary, then anything you add seems like the luxury it is.

A cynic might remark that nothing – absolutely nothing – that travels along the soil pipes of a domestic bathroom could begin to compare with the stuff industry, agriculture, and the controllers of toxic waste introduce to the environment daily.

The cynic would be right.

On the other hand there are at least two important things to be said in favour of cutting domestic pollution. One: every little helps, and if you think how many domestic bathrooms there are on the planet, it adds up to a formidable outpouring. Two: individuals who are going to some trouble to reduce their own waste are likely to be very intolerant of multinationals who are not, and there are occasions when intolerance is very healthy.

So if you really want to be environmentally friendly behind the washroom door, cut back.

Start with the water. Some modern lavatory cisterns give the option of full or half-flush, old-fashioned ones don't. There are those who advocate putting a brick in them to cut down water-use, but this isn't a brilliant idea because the brick tends to sprout algae. The Green Catalogue (see Address List) sells a block for the purpose – one that won't corrode, rust or populate itself with micro-organisms – but an alternative is a strong, clean plastic bottle (small enough not to get in the way of the flush mechanism) with the label soaked off and clean stones and water inside to weight it down. Periodically, take it out, empty it, wash everything and start again.

Don't leave taps dripping, shower more often than you bath and turn the tap on and off as necessary when cleaning teeth, rather than let it run for several minutes.

Also, consider using gel toothpaste or one of the 'natural' herbal toothpastes because the waste from the titanium oxide which gives the other kind its white creamy look damages rivers, and eventually seas, by raising their acidity. It isn't actually what you spit down the plughole that causes the problem, it's the waste created when the paste is made. (The new plastic tubes are healthier than the old lead-based ones, but they are not yet biodegradable. However, they are unavoidable at the moment.)

Similarly, with coloured lavatory paper, the main problems are not caused when it's flushed away but when it's manufactured and bleaches and dyes are used to turn it dazzling white or dainty peach. So although it's good if the roll is made from recycled paper, it's better still if it's a rather dingy grey – unless a non-chlorine-based bleach has been used.

Robert Swan, who has walked to both the North and South Poles and is now an environmental troubleshooter, told The Independent *in March 1993: "I reckon the new heroes of exploration are not the guys who climb Everest backwards in their underpants. It's the company that pioneers a way of making environmentally sound lavatory paper."*

Whatever the manufacturers say on the pack (and most are already changing the wording), it is never OK to flush away sanitary pads or tampons. When the proportion of sewage that is untreated hits the river or sea, they will be there too, neither a healthy nor an attractive addition to the waterscape. (You can buy bags to tie them in securely – acceptable packaging – so they can be put in the bin.) The same applies to condoms and disposable nappies. Bin them.

If you shave, you would not be surprised to be asked to avoid using a badger bristle shaving brush – but you might be surprised to be advised that an electric plug-in razor can use less energy than is expended in the manufacture of the plastic throw-away kind, especially if you get through a lot of them. It also means you don't need shaving foam, or a brush of any kind, and it avoids the use of batteries.

Bodies are not the only things that need to be cleaned – there are clothes, too. As far as possible, avoid wearing things that need to be dry-cleaned in toxic substances, and if you're using a washing-machine, go for a full load on a cool wash or else you're using too much power and powder and water. Powder (or liquid-wash) should be phosphate-free – this means it will foam less, but it will also pollute less.

GUESS WHOSE MUM DOESN'T USE GREEN WASHING POWDER?

SHINE
GLEAM GLEAM
GLOW GLOW
DAZZLE

USE NEW GREENO® WASHING POWDER FOR WHITES THAT ARE EASIER TO LOOK AT

Washing powder tends to stand in the same part of the shop or supermarket as other household cleaners. Many of these can cause problems, and it's worth remembering that it was perfectly possible to live in a sparklingly clean house before any of them were invented.

However, before making too many announcements to the effect that cookers can be cleaned with baking soda and water, windows with scrunched up newspaper dipped in vinegar and water, and the bath with half a lemon dipped in borax, consider who is actually going to have to do all this.

If it's you, then go to it and prove how effective it is. If it's someone else, then it's hardly fair to put on the pressure.

The point about modern cleaning fluids and creams – indeed, the very reason they were developed – is that they're effective, rapid and work with the minimum of physical effort on the part of whoever is using them. Their toxic, corrosive or other undesirable properties are an unfortunate side-effect.

Equally, energy-and-water-greedy washing-machines have released numerous people (usually women) from hours of boring, back-aching, hand-roughening, nail-breaking labour.

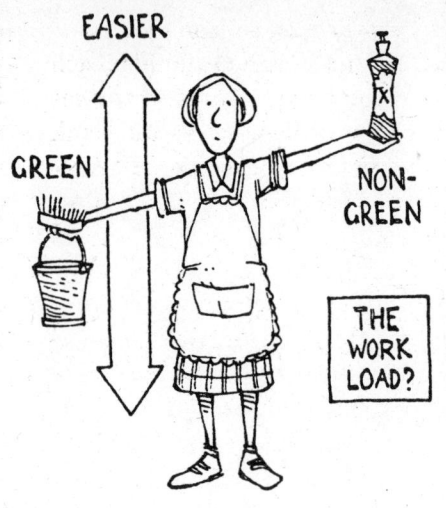

Take all that on if you're willing, but don't dish it out!

You're on safer ground mentioning that beeswax polish is better for the furniture, better for the beekeepers (who have to be environmentally friendly or their bees die), and doesn't come in aerosols. And that mothballs are toxic and room fresheners usually come in aerosols and are full of dubious chemicals, but dried lavender (or any other fragrant herb) works just as well. And that the Ecover range of cleaners is OK. And that kettle descalers are positively beneficial because a furred-up electric kettle uses more power than a clean one.

Also, that household bleach (which can't be used anyway if you have a septic tank because it destroys the bacteria that break down the sewage) may be a good disinfectant but is only rarely necessary. In the average home, using bleach is definitely over-kill. If anyone around you is really determined to use it, it might be worth pointing out that it usually contains sodium hypochlorite which, if mingled injudiciously (and against the advice on the pack) with other household cleaners forms the type of chlorine gas that was used as a weapon in World War One.

Household cleaning can show up the parts that need repainting. Read the small print on the can. Titanium oxide, itself something of a pollutant, has replaced the lead in gloss paints (emulsion never needed lead, which was there to speed up the drying process), but watch out for the occasional appearance of mercury compounds in the pigments – and be wary of paints used by professional painters, they can be asbestos-based.

And finally, one more thought for the bathroom, where all this began: has it ever occurred to you that if all the packaging that came off everything you used during your ablutions in the course of a year was piled in the doorway, you might not be able to get out ever again?

WHAT YOU NEED

WHAT THERE IS

Chapter Twelve

GET TO LOOK GOOD

Or: Please don't tell me I have to dress in fig leaves.

The South American three-toed sloth, although basically a rather boring beige colour, wears an attractive coating of green algae. For added interest, moths lay eggs in its hair and the feeding caterpillars form a kind of living jewellery. However, it is more than unlikely that these are a fashion statement – the rainforest's version of grunge. The sloth is so slow on the uptake, and so totally uninterested in personal daintiness, that it probably doesn't even know they are there.

Hermit crabs, which clamp themselves into empty whelk shells rather than grow their own, frequently decorate them with bits of weed and the occasional sea anemone. The effect is often very pretty, but the intention is camouflage, not ornamentation.

It seems that the human animal is the only one deliberately to change the colour of its hair or certain bits of its skin, to pierce holes in itself from which to hang bits of metal, to garland itself with mollusc acne (more commonly known as pearls) or the skeletons of tiny sea creatures (coral), to splash itself with bottled smells, and to drape itself with the skins and teeth of other animals. To be fair, it is a naked ape and it does need clothes. Unfortunately, it has never been very good at distinguishing between what it needs and what it wants.

> "One man's priority is another man's extravagance." Edwina Curry, *Three Line Quips* (Ashford, Buchan and Enwright 1992)

Actually, assembling a totally green wardrobe is not as straightforward as it might be. Natural fabrics – cotton and wool – are recommended, but neither is without problems.

Cotton is a greedy plant. It needs a lot of water and it takes so many nutrients out of the soil that cotton farmers feel obliged to feed it with quantities of chemical fertiliser. They also tend to use a lot of pesticides to make sure of a large and healthy crop.

(Genetic engineers are working to develop a cotton plant which is resistant to caterpillars and boll-weevil, and this could eventually cut the use of insecticides.)

Later on, the cotton is bleached, and usually dyed as well, both harmful procedures. (There are companies which have solved this by producing unbleached and undyed cotton clothes – some of which are made from organically-grown cotton – see Green Mail Order section of Address List.)

The only real problem with wool, apart from the dyeing, is that sheep are martyrs to ticks and other parasites. They have to be immersed regularly in toxic dips which eventually find their way into the soil and water.

Both cotton and wool, though, can be repaired and kept going longer than synthetic fabrics, and both can be recycled (old cotton clothes cut up so the best bits can be made into rag rugs or patchwork and the worst bits into kitchen cloths; baggy old wool jumpers unravelled and the yarn washed and reknitted, or woven into cheap tweed).

Real silk is probably not environmentally damaging (again, apart from dyes). If you can afford it, then whether or not you're happy to wear it depends on how you feel about its history. Caterpillars create the stuff for the specific purpose of building a secure cocoon within which to dissolve into a kind of insect-soup, re-form, and then emerge as a silk moth. Some people think it's distinctly unsporting to bake the cocoons at high temperature, killing the contents, and then unwind the silk and make it into handkerchiefs. Others don't think the insect-soup minds very much. Everyone has to make a personal decision on this.

Synthetic fabrics are frowned on because they are made from oil, which is a non-renewable resource. On the other hand, they're not entirely evil because they are often drip-dry so the energy that would have been used by the dryer and the iron is saved.

Until the clothes manufacturers catch up with the idea that it would be nice if the planet lasted longer than the latest fashion, the best anyone can do is not waste clothes. If you're bored with them, and they can't be recycled as suggested, perhaps they can be remodelled – different studs or buttons, sleeves from one thing swapped with sleeves from another (which could look strange but interesting), the colour changed with vegetable dyes, that kind of thing. Or take them to the local jumble sale or charity shop. (Most charity shops have arrangements with rag merchants, so it's worth taking clothes along even if they are not fit for anyone to wear.) And when you shop, don't forget to look first in the charity shop or jumble sale – it has to work both ways.

Also, try always to have clothes that wash because the dry-cleaning fluids used at the moment are noxious and dangerous. Some things that say 'Dry clean only' on the label can, in fact, be washed – extremely carefully and in pure soap powder. However, try out a small corner first – and bear in mind that if washing does do any damage, you can't complain to the supplier or the manufacturer (or to me).

When it comes to luxuries, the picture is slightly clearer. There are those who complain that environmentalists are always attacking the rich, and suggest this is only because they are mean-minded and jealous. The answer is that it is a simple fact that the rich are in a position to do far more harm than the poor – and also, possibly, more good.

You might think that the fight against the wearing of real fur had already been won. You would be wrong.

At the beginning of 1993, the Fur Education Council told The Guardian *newspaper that, despite the recession, fur sales during the previous year were up by at least 30%.*

You might also think you are not in a position to buy a fur. However, you may have influence with someone who is. And anyway, fur is not always made into full-length coats – there are gloves, and jacket trimmings, and hats.

I'M TRYING TO GO GREEN – MINE'S FAKE

The fur trade claims to be careful not to use the skins of endangered or protected species. In some places it lives up to this claim, but it must make mistakes – otherwise why are increasingly rare cheetahs, leopards and snow leopards, clouded leopards, jaguars, ocelots, lynx and tigers still mugged for their coats?

The fur trade also claims that the vast majority of skins used come from animals specially bred on ranches. They suggest that to breed and kill a silver fox for its pelt is no worse than to breed and kill a pig for its meat.

There is one anti-fur argument which agrees with this, and adds that the pig shouldn't be killed either. Another says that killing for luxury and killing for necessity are two totally different acts. A third points to the conditions in which ranch-fur animals are kept.

Fake fur, in common with other synthetic fibres, is oil-based.

Thoughts of fur lead to thoughts of leather. Poachers don't only hunt big cats, they go for reptiles, too. Crocodiles, caimans and alligators shared the earth with the dinosaurs but they may not be permitted to share it with us for much longer. We may perceive them as vicious – certainly they are dangerous – but they are also intelligent, brilliantly adapted for their swampy water life, and endangered.

It's impossible to justify attempting to turn entire species into expensive wallets, so people don't try, they just get on with it. And it's not only the crocodilians which suffer – lizards, snakes and anything else which has an attractive skin is at risk.

If cattle are to be killed for meat, it would be daft not to tan their hides for leather. If an animal is to die in the service of humanity, then every part of it should be used. A great many people find the wearing of this kind of leather acceptable – but if you are one of them, spare a thought for how it's cleaned. Methyl chloroform – or 1.1.1-trichlorethan – is frequently used for the specialised cleaning of suede and leather clothes.

Then there's jewellery. To start with the cheaper stuff –

plastic is oil-based, but there are a lot of attractive pieces around made from recycled plastic. At least one company specialises in earrings made from shaped and painted pieces of milk carton, which are much nicer than they may sound. (One sells through the Green Catalogue, see Address List.)

Wooden jewellery is all right if it's made from off-cuts of renewable timber. Garden trees need regular pruning, and because jewellery pieces are relatively small, this wood can be used, too.

These things can be bought, but most of them could be made at home – though you'd need to buy the metal hooks and fittings.

Shell jewellery is risky. Picking up empty shells from a beach is fine, and if this is what you've done, there's no problem. But tropical shells are sometimes collected for resale by companies who make no distinction between those which have living inhabitants and those which are finished with. In fact they sometimes collect them by a vacuum method which takes in living shells, sea anemones, small crabs and anything else that's within suction range. Be extremely wary about buying shell jewellery – or tropical shells for the aquarium or the bathroom shelf.

There are similar problems with coral. Coral polyps are related to sea anemones, but unlike anemones they live in communities, building up a reef, only part of which is actually alive, but all of which is home to masses of other sea creatures and their food. Coral reefs are being blasted all the time for building materials and lime, and all we can do about that is complain. But they are also plundered for jewellery and for those attractive branching bits which, along with the shells, go in aquaria or display cabinets. Have nothing to do with them – help cut the demand.

Disposable wrist watches have been around for some time now. They are obviously wasteful and should be avoided – a watch that can be mended, if necessary, and kept going for years is better. Best of all are the solar-powered ones – not as expensive as you might think – or good old traditional clockwork.

It's well known that ivory is unacceptable, so there's no need to mention it. (Except to say that it should be all right to use the ivory from elephants that have died naturally. Sadly for those craftsmen who work with this kind of ivory, it has to be banned along with the rest. No customs official, or other law-enforcement officer, could possibly tell the difference – and if there is any demand for ivory at all, the poachers will inevitably move in.)

All the above arguments apply also to tortoiseshell.

When you go really up market, and consider precious stones and metals, you're talking serious damage. Diamonds – a form of crystallized carbon found in Kimberlite rock – are the most popular of all the gemstones.

> "About 250 tonnes of Kimberlite rock must be processed to produce a 1 carat polished stone of gem quality."
> British Museum of Geology

Diamond mines, whether open-cast or underground, lay large areas of land to waste, and gallons upon gallons of water are needed for the processing. Tracts of wetlands have been drained and left lifeless for the sake of expensive glitter (and, of course, for industrial diamonds).

Gold (which is used in dentistry, medicine and electronics as well as for jewellery) is very occasionally panned from shallow streams – the way cartoon characters do it – but more often it is mined in a big way and can create even more environmental damage than diamond mining.

> "To produce one troy ounce (31.3g) of gold . . . requires over 5000 litres of water, 759kWh of electrical power, explosives, chemicals . . ." Arthur Street and William Alexander, Metals in the Service of Man *(Penguin 1989, 9th edition)*

When mined, gold is always 'contaminated' with silver, and sometimes also with copper and mercury. Mercury – which is highly toxic and can be absorbed through the skin and breathed in as vapour – may also be used to separate the gold from the ore in a process called amalgamation. A more modern method – the 'cyanide process' – uses a dilution of potassium cyanide, also a powerful poison. Both these toxins eventually escape into the immediate environment – and sometimes travel further. *New Scientist* reported in September 1992 that "Dangerous levels of mercury have been detected in the Pantanal in southwestern Brazil, the world's largest wetland . . . the mercury is dumped into rivers that flow into the Pantanal by gold-miners who use it to extract the precious metal from silt . . ."

Most silver is produced by refining it out of gold, zinc, lead or even copper – the rest is mined as 'free-state' silver ore which is usually found in gold or copper mines. Copper mining doesn't improve an area any more than the other kinds, and again there is the danger of mercury contamination.

Also, a mine doesn't stand alone – there have to be new roads, processing plants, store rooms, living quarters, generators for electrical power . . .

Anyone who has turned pale while contemplating all this might like to think briefly about make-up – cosmetics.

This all comes back to animals again. Animal fats, glands and tissues are used in cosmetics – perhaps especially in perfumes. Also, cosmetics are tested on them.

The Draize test involves dripping compounds (usually shampoos and hair dyes) into rabbits' eyes to see if they inflict any damage.

For other tests rats, mice or guinea pigs have the components of various cosmetics rubbed into shaven patches of their skin to check for allergic or dangerous reactions. It seems unnecessary to mention that this is not reasonable human behaviour.

There are cosmetics which do not have any animal tissue of any kind in them. There are very, very few cosmetics which have never, in any form, at any time in the past, been tested on animals.

However, some, at least, of the cosmetic industry is trying to turn itself around. It is possible to buy a few products, no part of which has ever been tested on animals – a few more, no part of which has been tested on animals in the last ten years – and even more, no part of which has been animal-tested in the last five years (nor, in any of these cases, ever will be again).

The pioneer of all this was a company called Beauty Without Cruelty – with the Body Shop, Cosmetics To Go (see Address List) and a great many small and not especially well-known companies continuing the good work. Even some of the cosmetic giants and supermarket own-brands make some products which have never inconvenienced an animal. (Be wary of the new EU symbol awarded to products that meet certain environmental criteria. The committee found the whole question of animal-testing too complicated to cope with and decided to ignore it. This means that some cosmetics which carry the symbol may be animal-unfriendly. For this reason, it has been boycotted by some of the cosmetic companies who care about animals and the environment.)

Read the labelling – ask questions – consult the Green Consumer Guide – and you will find you can paint your face and vegetable-dye your hair almost any way you choose – and still look a rabbit in the eyes without blushing.

Chapter Thirteen

GET FED

Or: If I live entirely on lettuce will I become truly green?

A lot of people have a difficult relationship with food. Half the world doesn't have enough. The other half has too much, and feels so guilty about it that it tries to take all the pleasure out of eating by dieting and worrying.

Assuming that you are getting enough to eat, there are really only two major problems. One, what the food is doing to you. Two, what it has already done to the planet.

In general, shops and supermarkets are keen to please their customers, so it's useful if the customers know what they want and what they don't want. However, there is a crucial difference between being well-informed and being obsessive. Bear in mind that it is a mistake to think too deeply or too often about everything on your plate. Self-starvation is impractical and hiccups are tiring.

Furthermore – the producers, manufacturers and purveyors of foodstuffs are not engaged in a conspiracy to poison the entire population. They simply want to produce as much food as possible and to make sure that it doesn't rot or go rancid while it is gathered, processed, transported and stored on the shop shelves. (Oh – and they want to make money.) Unfortunately, some of the chemicals used to achieve all this have turned out to have unappealing side effects. Maybe enough has been said by others about battery chickens and intensive farming in general. If you think of the animals as animals the whole idea is horrible. If you think of them as food it isn't much nicer.

> According to Animal Aid, the average British meat-eater consumes, in an average life-time, 36 pigs, 36 sheep, 8 cows, and 550 chickens, ducks and turkeys.

Briefly — exceedingly cramped and sometimes dirty living conditions mean there is a strong possibility of disease. Once disease starts it spreads rapidly. To cope with this, the animals are injected with antibiotics, some of which may remain in the carcasses. Overuse of antibiotics has the inconvenient effect of training bacteria to become immune to them. And even after the use of antibiotics, large numbers of chickens and eggs are infected with salmonella, which is destroyed only by thorough cooking.

Also, animals are sometimes treated with growth hormones so their bodies build more meat in a shorter time. Hormone residues can still be present when the meat is sold and eaten.

They may be fed on extraordinary things, too. The minced-up carcasses of chickens which died from infections are sometimes dished up to other chickens. Also beef cattle (which are not natural carnivores, either) have occasionally been given the remains of infected sheep, disguised in cattle pellets. This is where BSE (Bovine Spongiform Encephalopathy) originated. BSE is a horrible affliction which causes the brain to turn spongy. Collapse and death inevitably follow. Even though experts assure us it cannot be transmitted to humans, reputable suppliers avoid using untested beef. In fact some countries ban British beef altogether. This is unnecessary because most of it is OK — but their caution is understandable.

Later, mass slaughtering makes hygiene difficult — especially when it comes to offal and what is rather unnervingly called 'mechanically recovered meat'. This last is a mixture of gristle and general ghastly bits which are removed from the stripped bones by machinery. Now — it's no use admiring tribal peoples for respecting the buffalo, or whatever, and for using every part of it, if at the same time you are going to refuse to eat any of the bullock apart from the obvious steak-type bits from the flank and shoulder. However, mechanically recovered meat — which usually goes into things like meat pies and sausages — can easily carry bacteria if it isn't dealt with in totally hygienic conditions. Also, because it is not in itself very appealing, it needs a lot of help from additives – colourings, flavourings and preservatives.

> "I would reduce the grazing of cattle and grow vegetables instead. If everyone in the world was vegetarian there would be enough food to feed the whole of the world's population." Anja B Fors, 16, Norway

PROBLEMATIC FISH

Fish can be problematic, too. Drift nets set for tuna frequently also catch dolphins and porpoises, which then either drown or are killed by the fishermen. Dolphins do not suffer when tuna are caught by line, and some companies are careful about this. The Whale and Dolphin Conservation Society say that they won't be convinced until an independent monitoring system has been set up. Unless the shop or supermarket, or the supplier, by way of labelling on the can, is able to convince you the tuna is dolphin friendly, it is probably best avoided.

An unexpected enemy can surface here – GATT. GATT is the General Agreement on Tariffs and Trade, an international treaty seeking to promote free trade worldwide, partly by controlling the right of the 108 member countries to limit imports. Under GATT, governments hold 'rounds' of talks, each of which can drag on for four years or more. Free and unrestricted world trade might sound good – but GATT can be invoked to prevent member countries banning the import of dolphin unfriendly tuna. (It can also prevent a poor country using import bans to protect its struggling industries from foreign competition.)

When it comes to other fish, there is no clear way of knowing if the catch came from polluted waters – nor is there much the individual can do about the fact that intensive over-fishing may be seriously depleting fish stocks. So don't worry about that.

Val Kilmer, star of Top Gun *and* The Doors, *says of his Cherokee ancestors:* "*They have this tradition of living not just for the next generation, but for seven generations – so that you don't completely fish out a lake, you move on*. *But of course that's completely alien to our 'I want it now' culture.*" Mail on Sunday (October 1992)

Fish farms are a way round the problem of over-fishing, although some of them also use growth hormones and few are entirely environmentally friendly. Keeping fish in unnaturally high numbers upsets the ecological balance of the area (it has been known for fish to die from overcrowding) and fish-food can cause algae blooms. Also fish farmers are in competition with predators – cormorants near the coast, herons inland. It is not unknown for a fish farmer to shoot a feeding heron – despite the fact that it is a fully protected bird. However, this is rare, and if you know of a fish-farmer suffering heron-attention, point out that the Royal Society for the Protection of Birds will advise on acceptable ways of keeping them at bay.

Given that there's not a lot to be gained by worrying about fish, you may as well concentrate on warm-blooded animals.

There are two obvious things to do about intensive farming (in addition to joining a pressure group and protesting about conditions).

One is to buy, or persuade whoever does the shopping to buy, free-range chickens, eggs from free-range hens, 'real meat' which has come from farms where the animals have been cared for properly, and have not been injected with unacceptable things (see The Real Meat Company in the Address List).

The other is to become a vegetarian.

But the vegetables can get you, too.

This might be the moment to mention that we live longer and are taller, larger, stronger and healthier than our ancestors.

At the beginning, there is

the soil, and in the soil there are fertilisers. Natural fertilisers, compost or manure, put back the nutrients that previous crops have taken out. Chemical fertilisers, which boost growth far more, often put back too much. Any that is not taken up by the plants remains in the soil and can leach out into streams and rivers where it overfeeds the algae and weeds until they get overgrown and out of control.

Then there are fungicides which destroy moulds, pesticides which destroy insects, and herbicides which kill weeds. None of these have a very positive effect on wildlife. Some, especially 'good' insects, are killed directly. Others have their foodplants destroyed or their food chain disrupted.

Some of these chemicals are removed when the food is washed or prepared – except for the 'systematic pesticides' which are absorbed into the plant and become a part of it.

When the harvested food is stored, it needs to be held in a sort of time-warp so that it doesn't sprout, or over-ripen, or grow mould. In some countries, including Britain, methyl bromide – one of the CFCs – is used to do this.

If the food is made into cakes, pies, drinks, jams, crisps, fish fingers, ready-meals, etc, things will be added to it. Additives. E numbers.

Not everybody is aware of E numbers. Those who are tend to react to them with wild-eyed fear, as if every E carried a skull and crossbones symbol. It's wise to be careful, but before terror gets a grip, think of two things. One – not all additives are evil. Two – even the most disagreeable ones are only present in tiny quantities.

All E numbers must be shown on the label.

Once you get additives in perspective, there is still irradiation – the use of gamma rays to kill bacteria in fresh food. This is, of course, supposed to be harmless. Certainly it doesn't mean your carrots will glow in the dark.

On the positive side, it is reassuring to think of bacteria being done to death, and also it could cut down the use of chemical preservatives.

On the negative side, environmental groups are

against it. They point out that the vitamin content of the food – usually fresh fruit or veg – is sometimes reduced and that the long-term effects are not known. They also think that a good standard of hygiene should make it unnecessary anyway. Cynics imply that it's a neat way of using up nuclear waste.

There *is* something rather creepy about it – mainly because, as yet, there isn't any labelling to tell you whether or not your food has had this particular experience. However, you can ask the supermarket.

One answer to all this is to buy organically grown fruit and vegetables, if they're available and if you can afford them, despite the fact that they may be smaller, oddly shaped, and discreet in colour, unlike the large, perfectly formed sort, in their cheery story-book colours.

It may be pointed out to you that yields of organically grown vegetables are lower, and there are a lot of people to feed. This is true. It is also true that in order to keep the price of commercially grown fruit and veg high enough, the EU regularly destroys the surplus. So yields are already too high – and government funding of organic growers could ensure that they make a reasonable living.

> "Once caught or harvested, food should be eaten by human beings and not ruined by paint or burnt for economic reasons." Tina Korsgaard Gertz, 17, Denmark

And there is now one more piece of science fiction which has become a science fact – genetic engineering. The genetic engineer uses sophisticated techniques to change the genetic make-up of an organism. The point of this is to produce particular characteristics; for example plants that can resist insect predators (cutting the need for pesticides) or which are especially fruitful (cutting the need for artificial fertilisers).

There are no plans, so far, to mention this on labelling.

"[The] important advantage of genetic engineering is that it provides the very latest technology to farmers in a very traditional package – the seed. Even the most impoverished nations will thus have access to the benefits without the need for high-technology sup-

plies or costly materials.''
Charles S Gesser and Robert T Fraley, Scientific American *(June 1992)*

The idea of modifying food plants to improve the crop isn't at all new. Farmers and gardeners have been doing it for thousands of years – by saving the seeds from the best. More recently, cross-breeding of plants has become quite common. What *is* new is the ability of scientists to unravel the genetic code of organisms and then interface with it to create – artificially – different characteristics.

So even if genetic engineering is just one more step on the agricultural road, it's a big step.

Some people worry that traditional crops may be allowed to die out. Others are nervous in case all food-plants and animals somehow end up belonging to the few multinational companies who can afford to fund the research. Many simply don't like the idea of Dr Frankenstein tampering with their grub.

It's already happening, though. Most of us have probably enjoyed a genetically engineered tomato – tomatoes are said to be very easy-going about this sort of treatment. And anyone who has eaten vegetarian cheese has gratefully consumed some genetically-engineered rennet. ('Normal' rennet, which is what makes cheese go solid, is taken from the fourth stomach of a dead calf.)

When you eventually get the food home and unwrap it, consider the packaging. Is there too much? If so, is that your fault or theirs? If it's yours, what are you going to do about it? If it's theirs, are you going to tell them?

Finally, a quick note about fast food.

This is often frowned on. The big beef about burgers is that they increase demand for meat, and an excess of cattle causes all kinds of damage. Areas of rainforest are cut down, either to provide grazing land, or to grow soya as animal-feed when it would make more sense to feed the soya straight to humans. Also, cows fart methane, a greenhouse gas – and more herds mean more hot air. At the restaurants themselves, there is a great deal of packaging which means waste and litter and sometimes CFCs.

On the plus side, at least one of the major hamburger chains insists that it does not encourage the destruction of virgin rainforest for new ventures, but only buys meat from established ranches. Also, it funds the planting of new trees and is beginning to use recycled, and/or recyclable packaging. It doesn't comment on the farts or the soya-animal-feed, but its kitchen hygiene is good.

In the end, the customer is in charge. You are within your rights to ask where the meat comes from and what the packaging is made of, and to let them know that you would like less packaging and more vegeburgers.

Every shop, every supermarket, every restaurant, fast or not, is only there because enough customers support it. If the customers demand reasonable changes, these will be made. Go for it.

Bon appetit.

Chapter Fourteen

GET RID...

Or: Slipping off a banana skin.

It's difficult to think of a more elegant form of packaging than the banana skin – strong and protective, bright and attractive, easy to open. As it developed long before the invention of tarmac and paving slabs its slippery qualities can't logically be regarded as a design fault.

Coconut shells are even more impressive, although you have to bear in mind, when they resist every possible assault with hammer, chisel or machete and you're considering trying to borrow a sub-machine gun, that you're actually not supposed to be able to get into them.

Considering that almost every living thing is encased in some form of packaging – bark, seed-case, skin, carapace, shell, scale, hide (with additional fur, hair or feather) – it's remarkable that we didn't get seriously over-excited about the possibilities until roughly fifty years ago.

In a civilisation where foods and other consumer goods are usually grown or made huge distances from where they are bought or consumed, some packaging is clearly essential. It would be difficult (though interesting) to try to transport litreloads of carbonated liquids, several thousand flakes of cereal, or fifty personal stereos from factory to shop except in containers. A shelf-ful of canned baked beans without the cans would not be a pretty sight.

Packaging protects and makes handling possible. The right packaging keeps food fresh for longer, makes freezing possible, and also shows if food has been tampered with; useful when the occasional social misfit threatens to poison large numbers of strangers unless enormous sums of money are made instantly available. (The money never is made available, and the entrepreneurs are usually caught, but it's reassuring to be able to check whether or not they got at the food first.)

Also, packaging can look good. Unfortunately, this has led to the curious belief that more packaging looks even better.

The increase is achieved in various ways. There's the highly successful Miniaturisation Method. This involves putting edibles into tiny snack-sized packs, none of which ever contains quite enough, so that everyone feels compelled to buy at least two. An extension of this method is to offer several snack-sized packs inside a large one. (Buy in bulk if you can.)

There's the Surreal Method – packaging something which quite obviously doesn't need it. Even coconuts, with their famously heavy-duty natural packaging, have been observed encased in clingwrap. (Buy unwrapped fruit and veg where possible.)

And there's the Let's-Not-Try-To Be-Subtle-Let's-Just-Go-For-It Method. You know this one's in operation when you buy something electrical and discover that it's stowed away in bubblewrap within a styrofoam container, that the styrofoam container is parcelled up in cellophane, that the cellophane parcel has been slipped inside an attractively designed box, and that the box itself is protected by shrink-wrap. The ultimate is when the whole thing is engulfed in tissue paper and put into a plastic carrier bag. (Refuse the carrier and complain about the rest.) Whoever buys all this packaging (together with whatever was in it) eventually has to get rid of it, somehow and somewhere. Usually the whole lot goes out with the rubbish, household waste, garbage, trash, or whatnot – forming almost thirty per cent of the total.

> "Most Americans will leave behind a monument of waste some 4,000 times their bodyweight by the time they die. (For Europeans the figure is 1,000 times – for Madagascans, 100 times). To put it another way, the United States produces some 180 million tons of waste a year." From Central TV documentary 'Sex, Lemurs, and Holes in the Sky' (17 November 1992)

It might be possible to calculate that of all the people lying on their backs on the floor listening to Heavy Metal on the stereo and eating individually wrapped chocolate biscuits, 78% are not thinking about anything at all; and that of the 22% who are, only .0005% of them are pondering the ultimate fate of the wrappers.

For the benefit of that .0005%, the answer is that they are likely to be buried in a landfill site, in the company of a large and complex mix of other things, where they will rot down and give off methane gas, which will eventually contribute to the greenhouse effect – if it doesn't explode first.

Methane or marsh gas (CH_4): colourless, odourless hydrocarbon gas produced by natural wetlands, stagnant water, paddy fields, rotting organic matter, animal excreta, natural gas. Explosive when mixed with 7 or 8 parts oxygen (O) in restricted space (coalmine, landfill site). Can ignite to produce 'will o' the wisp' effect. One of the so-called greenhouse gases. May be used as energy source.

As it has already been established that large quantities of nuclear, chemical and other toxic waste, not to mention untreated sewage, are regularly dumped in unsuitable places, can it really be true that a surplus of candy-wrappers is a serious problem? Well, given the size of the surplus, yes. Also, the point of going on about packaging is that a lot of it doesn't need to be there. If we could all cut down on that, and then cut down on the rest of the stuff we get rid of, the positive effect on the planet would be significant.

Traditionally, at any rate in the UK, domestic rubbish is not sorted before being buried (or burned, which can create noxious fumes, ingredients for acid rain, and yet more greenhouse gas). And domestic rubbish is not all candy wrappers, cat food cans and the remains of take-away Vindaloo. There is also what tends to be known as Hazardous Household – dregs of paint, varnish and stripper, sump oil, batteries, medicines, aerosols . . .

There are seven methods of domestic toxic waste disposal: dumping in landfill

105

sites, burying deep underground, dumping at sea, discharging into the sewers, burning, subjecting to chemical treatment, re-using or recycling. In the UK, most of it goes into landfill sites.

However, the Department of Trade and Industry, the Department of the Environment and several local councils – most notably Leeds – are already aware of the problems, and Leeds was first to take action. Their pilot scheme – in which they provided a one-off Hazardous Household collection – showed that people would be willing to co-operate if such schemes were available nationwide. It's true they're expensive, but maybe a tax could be levied on toxins to offset the cost?

In the meantime, we could all attempt to organise our lives so we don't have anything grisly to get rid of in the first place. If for some reason your lifestyle forces you to surround yourself with unwanted poisons, contact your local council for advice.

Old medicines can go back to the chemist. If there is a Family Health Service Association scheme in operation in the area, the chemist can arrange to have the drugs safely disposed of locally. If not, they will be returned to the pharmaceutical company or, in the case of Boots, back to Head Office, which will arrange for them to be incinerated. They can't be recycled because no one can be sure how long you've had them or where you stored them.

Batteries are a problem because they may contain toxic heavy metals – mercury, cadmium or lead – though it's true that many have been reformulated to omit these, but it is still better to avoid using them. If you must use them, try to go for rechargeables (and invest in a recharger). An EU Directive of summer 1993 says that the EU is aiming for "the gradual reduction of spent batteries in household waste". But it's a complicated process because how do you get people to take them to collection points? How long can they be stored there before they leak and the leakings mingle and become dangerous? And how do you make it cost-effective and energy-efficient to recycle them?

Lead-acid batteries (as in cars) are, obviously, rechargeable. When they've finally had it, the manufacturers will usually take them back. The easiest way to get them to the manufacturer is by way of the retailer – (some retailers are helpful, some not). Scrap merchants are another possibility. Not much, yet, is done about the small lead-acid batteries used in security alarm systems, because they have little scrap value. An estimated 4,000 tonnes of these is junked each year.

Nickel cadmium batteries (which come in three forms and are used in shavers, camcorders, computers etc) may be reclaimed and recycled soon (under the same EU Directive).

There are at the moment no clear plans for dealing with the less dangerous batteries – used in torches, toys, cameras, radios, personal stereos and so on.

There are plans in the making to mark each type of battery with its specific heavy-metal content and to set up massive collection and recycling schemes – but these would be expensive and difficult to put into operation. Until something comes of this, you could try returning spent ones to the supplier or manufacturer. (It's possible they will simply dump them in their own trash, but you will have made a point.)

In fact, of course, very little domestic waste is specifically toxic, it's just that there's such an astonishingly enormous amount of it and there need not be. If weeds are just flowers in the wrong place, then most rubbish is just matter in the wrong place.

A proportion of packaging would be more useful if it had remained in the trees it came from. Complain about it.

> "If I ruled the planet, I'd abolish garbage dumps. The only reason we seem over-run with garbage is because we classify more and more objects *as* garbage. What *is* garbage? It varies between individuals. The old pail you throw out might be very useful to a fisherman looking for a place to store his bait." Ben Duffus, 18, Canada

Plastic carrier bags are almost never necessary – also they're as slithery as a banana skin and bite into your fingers when they're full. Get a basket or a canvas bag or something. If you have to accept a plastic bag, re-use it, or give it to a charity shop which will re-use it for you.

Things which are made to be used once, or only for a short time, and then chucked out (single-use cameras, non-repairable watches, paper knickers) are designed to cost you more money than you realise. Avoid them.

Unless you have spent the last ten years off the planet (possibly on a space station attempting to study the enormous invisible mass known as The Great Attractor, towards which the Milky Way, in company with several other galaxies, is said to be moving at an estimated speed of 600 km per second) you will have spotted the arrival of bottle banks. You will therefore already know that recycling glass is now possible in many parts of the UK. (Don't forget glass jars can go in the same place.) This saves not just the raw material (sand) but energy (a lot). As it happens, re-using the bottles would be even more energy-efficient (bring back the returnable bottle) but this will do for now.

You are also likely to know the value of recycling paper. The European paper-making industry is already adapting its technology to use paper-pulp as a raw material and is looking at ways of avoiding using chlorine bleaches which leach dioxins into the rivers. They are becoming increasingly flexible – producing high-quality papers (often using part-recycled paper, part-woodpulp) as well as lower-grade kitchen and lavatory paper. Many local councils will collect used paper (not coloured paper, as in magazines, and not anything with glue in it, as in telephone directories) – or ask your local branch of Friends of the Earth for news of schemes near you.

Plastics recycling is newish, but building. In the UK, The British Plastics Federation is co-ordinating efforts and publishing Fact Sheets to reassure environmentalists that plastics manufacturers have a sense of responsibility about what they produce. This is nice – but actions are better than reassurances.

The scrap created by the industry itself is almost always recycled, and so is some plastic reclaimed from commercial or industrial users.

Domestic plastic waste is more of a problem because it's expensive to collect, sort into the different types, and send off to the relevant recycling plant. It would be counter-productive to use up too much non-renewable energy collecting and recycling it all. However, a few plastic-bottle banks are already in place and there are kerbside collections of domestic plastic waste in several towns and cities in the US, Canada, and Europe (including Britain). Also, two of the major polystyrene manufacturers are developing their own recycling techniques – and there are pilot schemes for the collection of vending machine cups.

The plastics recycling figures are not hugely impressive (less than 10% of the annual UK output) but it's a beginning. So if there is a waste-plastic collection scheme near you, use it. It'll only work if the majority of people co-operate.

> "If I ruled the planet, I would introduduce laws to make companies use recycled materials in their products, thus creating a market for the material." Perry Quinton, 18, Canada

Abandoned vegetation (potato peelings, the outside leaves of cabbages, strawberry hulls) is not a problem for anyone with a garden. Pile it all in a corner (maybe dig a shallow hole first) where it can rot down to form a natural and free fertiliser. There are things you can do to speed up the rotting down process, or to enrich the eventual mixture, but it will work even if you don't.

If you wish, you can call your pile of unwanted vegetation a compost heap. Be warned, though, that if you do you will find you attract all kinds of advice. This should help you to create the best compost heap in your hemisphere, on the other hand it might unnerve you. If all you want is to turn leftover leaves and stalks into plant food, then call it something else and go for it. (Later, when you're committed to it, seek sensible advice from the Soil Association or the Henry Doubleday Research Association, see Address List.) One other word of warning, compost heaps can attract rats.

If you don't have a garden, check if your local council runs a compost collection. (If you live in Leeds the answer is that they do.) If not, you just have to throw it all away.

Almost everyone knows scrap metal is worth money – not everyone knows that aluminium cans are. More than that, recycling the metal is relatively easy and extremely helpful. Aluminium, the most abundant of the world's metals, is extracted from bauxite which is mined from granite rocks in Australia, Brazil and Jamaica, among other places. It takes an enormous amount of energy to compel four tonnes of bauxite to yield one tonne of aluminium. It seems short-sighted in the extreme to go through all this to create a substance which is already available, rolling about mournfully in city street and school playground. Also, the energy used to recycle aluminium is only a fifth of the energy used to mine and process it from scratch.

Contact Alcan (see Address List) for an information pack on what to do. (The bottom line is – you collect aluminium cans and sell them to a merchant who pays by weight.) Over 50% of drinks cans in the UK are aluminium (the figure is higher in the US where recycling is mandatory in some states). You can check by doing a kind of reverse test with a magnet – if it sticks to the magnet, it isn't. Contact the Steel Can Recycling Information Bureau (see Address List) for advice on what to do with the other kind. It may not seem worthwhile for a single household to start a collection – but a group of households could get together, and possibly join in with a local school or college. Alternatively, check if the local authority has can banks.

(If you have to store them for a while until you're ready to dispose of them, it might be worth investing in a small can-crusher. Otherwise you'll be storing more air than metal.)

Used cooking foil, milk bottle tops and the containers from pre-cooked and take-away food can also be saved. The Aluminium Foil Recycling Campaign (see Address List) is currently setting up pilot schemes with 50 local authorities in Britain. The Charities Aid Foundation (see Address List) has published a modestly priced booklet which tells you where to take or send foil and bottle tops, and also other things which are not usually thought of as recyclable – like used greetings cards, magazines, spectacles, wrist watches, video games, computer software, and so on.

And finally –

This is reality.

You cannot throw anything away.

You can only mend it and keep it – or change it into some other thing – or use it for some other purpose – or put it in some other place.

Or not buy it in the first place.

"We need less luxury and waste in a few countries so there can be less poverty and hunger in the greater part of the world." Fidel Castro of Cuba, speaking to *The Observer* (14 June 1992)

Chapter Fifteen
GET SWITCHED ON AND REVV'D UP

Or: I'm not really green, I'm just car sick.

If you'd like to spice up your life with a little paranoia, read on.

If fear gives you a buzz, forget old friends – Dracula and the undead, werewolves, witches, and demonic apparitions. Forget the sinister sound in the cellar and the dark at the top of the stairs. Forget Freddie Kruger ... Cars are the modern monsters.

Cars are trying to kill us, and very few people seem to have noticed.

Each year a typical car produces 4000kg of carbon dioxide, 300kg of carbon monoxide, 20kg of nitrogen oxides and 50kg of hydrocarbons. These don't just go into the air, they go into the water and food as well. UK petrol also has about 5% benzene (the figure is lower in the US). Benzene is known to be carcinogenic (it can cause cancer) and you get more of it if you are driving the car or truck than the people outside do.

Cars and trucks pollute the air, the water and the food.

The Department of Environment has a free telephone line (0800 556677) on which a friendly recorded voice will tell you about the air quality over various parts of Britain on the day of your call. If the quality is bad, the voice will recommend that people with breathing problems should avoid strenuous exercise and that children with asthma should be kept back from games.

It's nice to be warned. What's annoying is that no one seems to ask those who are causing the problem to do anything about it; it's the sufferers who are expected to change their routines and mess up their social lives. (To be fair, some cities, including Cambridge, Zurich, Geneva, Stuttgart and Cologne, now ban cars and trucks in their centres.)

It wouldn't be strictly accurate to say that cars breed like rabbits, but they do multiply very rapidly.

> "The number of cars in the UK is growing by about 500,000 every year."
> Transport 2000

In a city during rush hour it can seem as though all 500,000 of the extras are simultaneously fuming at a standstill.

Yet although we can see there are already too many of them for the roads to carry, we don't try to limit their numbers. Instead, we build new roads and widen old ones.

Tarmac is laid where tarmac never was (there goes another bit of countryside; part of a village, perhaps, or maybe a strip of ancient woodland, downland or wetland).

The more roads we build, and the wider we build them, the more cars there will be. The London Orbital, the M25, was already inadequate by the time it had opened. It was not unique in this. Clearly there is a problem – but it can't be solved in one go. We cannot instantly outlaw the car.

Two years ago, the 700,000 members of German Greenpeace tried to survive for a month without using a car at all. They each managed to cut down car-use, but only 5,000 or so succeeded in giving it up altogether. This does not mean the majority of German Greenpeace members are failures – it means the problem is too complicated at the moment for even the best-intentioned people to solve it rapidly.

> "If I ruled the planet I would introduce a car-free Sunday once a month. On this day public transport would be free, or at least cheaper. There would also be enough buses and trains running to get (nearly) everywhere." Bettina Keuchel, 19, Germany

The whole structure of our lives and our living areas is designed on the assumption that most of us drive cars (or live with people who drive cars). There are people in outlying towns in the US, as in small towns and villages in Britain, who have no other means of getting to work, to school, to the shops or anywhere else. No regular system of public transport serves them. It is too far, and perhaps not safe, to walk.

What we need to aim for is a different pattern of living.

Instead of planning huge out-of-town supermarkets with giant car-parks, we should be bringing the supermarkets into urban areas, using them to perk up rundown inner-city sites.

We should also be buying at least some of what we need from small, local shops. Village shops all over Britain have died from lack of custom. If the majority of people climb into their hatchbacks and roar off to the hypermarket, there will never be enough customers to enable a small shop to survive. This makes life extraordinarily difficult for people without cars – unless they live right in a town or city. It also means that villages and small towns have lost a lot of their character and vitality.

Instead of investing in massive road-building, we should be doing something about public transport – subsidising it until we have a cheap, efficient, safe and integrated system that people are willing to use. Something which will actually take them where they want to go, when they want to go, and then bring them back again.

> "When we rule the planet we'll stop the use of the car. Instead of the state giving money to the military, it will support public transport. This will reduce the output of CO_2 gases." Signe Eide and Marte Graff Jenssen, both 15, Norway

It's true that buses are as guilty as cars when it comes to giving off fumes, but one bus with sixty people on it is better than sixty cars with one person in each. Trains use energy, but because of the numbers they can carry they are far more energy-efficient than cars, and infinitely less polluting. Trams, which also use power but are relatively fume-free, have already been reintroduced in one or two places in Britain, France and the US.

In Europe and the US, manufacturers are attempting to produce electrically powered cars. Electric milk floats have been a familiar sight for a long time, but though their top speed is quite adequate for their purpose, it isn't acceptable to anyone with a modern sense of urgency. Also, at the moment, not even the most powerful available battery will last out for a long journey.

California, with its policy of aiming for zero emissions, is roaring ahead with electric car production. It will be interesting to see the results – but it seems unlikely that electric cars are going to be the whole answer. Although it's true that they don't give out pollution as they travel, batteries are toxic, and the power to charge them still has to come from somewhere. Unless it is coming from a power station running on solar power (or wind or wave energy), then the pollution is simply being moved back along the production line.

It is possible for the internal combustion engine to run on fuel other than petrol. (It is said that, at a push, it can use chicken droppings, but that seems unlikely to become a popular option.) Research continues into non-petroleum-based fuels, among them ethanol. Ethanol is a form of alcohol which can be extracted from oilseed rape, among other plants. However, as things are at the moment, if ethanol were to replace petrol an astonishing amount of the Earth's surface would have to be given over to growing the crops from which it can be produced.

Any of these lines of research may lead somewhere. It's even possible that someone will come up with something entirely new. The internal combustion engine was entirely new, once.

Until the technology changes, though, we have to function with what we've got. We cannot get rid of the car-monster, not yet anyway, but some attempts can be made to tame it.

It's common knowledge that every car should be fitted with a catalytic converter and run on unleaded petrol. This is some help – but not nearly as much as most people seem to think. Environmentalists tend to be sceptical about catalytic converters. They are grimly aware that too many people genuinely believe that a catalytic converter can turn vehicle emissions into pure air, or something very like it.

A car with a catalytic converter is not environmentally friendly – it is just marginally less unfriendly. The catalytic converter will reduce the toxicity of the emissions from the exhaust, but it will not cut out the carbon dioxide. What is more, it won't begin to work until the engine has warmed up, so on a short trip it probably doesn't function at all.

> There is no such thing as a green car – unless it has no engine and is being used as a hen-house.

What you have to do is use the car less. And less still. And don't leave the engine running unnecessarily. And learn to drive well. Sudden braking, sudden acceleration and high speed all use more fuel and all give off more CO_2.

It is extraordinary how many people who are physically capable of walking, don't. It's weird how many people, with full use of all their limbs, will take a car to the local library, swimming pool, shops or pizza parlour. Sometimes it's so hard for them to find anywhere to park that the walk from the parking-place is almost the same length as the walk from home would have been.

> "If I ruled the planet, I would outlaw cars. There would only be public transportation. That way there would be less carbon dioxide... plus people would be in better health because they would need to walk more." Anne Keenan, 15, US

And there are other wheels – there are bicycles. Although a mountain bike can do untold damage in the wrong place – on a woodland trail, for example – it is ideal for local travel. Or it would be, if the cars were better controlled and safe cycle-lanes were provided everywhere. As it is, in some areas it's simply too dangerous.

If there are any journeys you can safely make on foot or by bike, go for it. If that's not practical, take the public transport option ahead of the car option. But remember this: if you care enough to try to make changes, your planet needs you. Do not take risks.

If you do have a bicycle, or are thinking of getting one, you might consider joining a group of some kind. The largest national cycling organisation in Britain is the CTC (Cyclist's Touring Club) which campaigns for better facilities for cyclists, organises cycling tours throughout Europe and advises members on choosing and maintaining their machines.

As well as other wheels, there are also other fuels – diesel and CNG, for instance.

Diesel-fuel has no lead in it and diesel engines are more fuel-efficient than petrol engines. However, diesel still emits carbon monoxide, hydrocarbons and nitrogen oxides. It also gives off particulates – bits of unburnt carbon (otherwise known as smuts) which are small, dirty and possibly carcinogenic (cancer-inducing).

CNG (compressed natural gas) emits far less CO_2 than petrol, no lead, hardly any particulates and doesn't cause any photo-chemical smog. Nothing's perfect though, and it does have limitations, not least of which is that the fuel tank has to be four or five times the size of a standard petrol tank. Also it's expensive to distribute (it'll be a long time before it's available in every service station) and it is likely to give off methane – a greenhouse gas.

However, it clearly has major advantages over petrol, and is currently being tried out in numerous towns and cities, mostly for buses and delivery vans.

(People who were worried that CNG-powered vehicles might blow up if involved in accidents were somewhat reassured when a serious fire in a Dutch garage passed off without a single explosion.)

The biggest CNG scheme in Europe is in Göteborg, Sweden, where the buses (with their gas tanks on their roofs) have specially designed mono-fuel engines which give out the least possible emissions. (Engines which can also run on petrol, as a back-up, are more likely to emit nasties, even when running on CNG.) CNG is also used in Copenhagen, Helsinki, Oslo, Stockholm, Nantes, San Diego, Los Angeles, Pittsburgh, Detroit and Houston, among other places. In New Zealand 80% of taxis and buses run on it, and there are schemes in Argentina, Indonesia, Thailand, Pakistan and Russia (though unfortunately the Russian pipeline tends to leak methane). There are plans to introduce CNG in other countries, including the UK.

Something completely different which might ease traffic congestion would be if far more of the people who could work from home, did. It is beginning to happen – but not yet enough to make much difference. Someone whose job is in a shop, power station, hospital or factory – someone who drives a bus or maintains telephone lines or teaches in a school or college – has to go out to work. But now that there are computers with modems, telephones and faxes, many people who work in offices could probably function very well from home, with perhaps an occasional trip in to central-command.

This introduces a whole other power problem – the over-use of energy.

When we first worked out how to make fire, we only needed it to cook our food and keep us warm. Now look!

We use energy for air-conditioning and fans, for central heating and fires, for water-heating and lighting (at home, at work, in the street . . .); for cooking with hobs and ovens, with rotisseries, microwaves and toasters, and to electrify kettles and coffee makers; for labour-saving devices like washing machines, driers, blenders, mixers, grinders, power tools, electric carving knives and scissors, irons and vacuum cleaners; for music centres and stereos, televisions, videos, computers, telephones with all possible attachments; for hair driers, shavers and Christmas tree decorations . . .

It's so easy. Just press the switch and it's there. If you had to go out and buy it and then carry it home again, you'd be more careful with it. If it was rare and hard to find, you'd be downright stingy with it. But, in most parts of Europe and the US, and in many other places worldwide, it is readily available – and unless you have the kind of meter that has to be fed with coins, it almost seems to be free.

Yet, unless the power source is some kind of renewable energy (solar, wind, wave etc), then the generation of every kilowatt you use has been directly responsible for atmospheric pollution.

Renewable energy is already available in some places, but at the moment it only provides a fraction of the amount we use daily. Long-term, we need to work towards creating more of it. Short-term, we have to use less.

The US electronics firm Intel has developed a micro-processor technology which means their computers only use about 10% of power when switched on but not in use. But HDTV (High Definition Television) is in a high street store near you – and one HDTV set uses approximately four times the electric current used by an ordinary TV.

Everybody knows how to use less electricity – it's simply a question of whether or not they're willing to do it.

Do you use more hot water than you need?

Do you leave lights on in empty rooms? Do you use old-fashioned high-energy light bulbs instead of modern low-energy ones (which burn as brightly but last about eight times longer and use 75% less power)?

Are you running appliances off batteries (energy-intensive in the making, toxic when disposed of) even though you would use less power if you plugged into the mains?

Do you turn up the central heating to save yourself the enormous inconvenience of putting on an extra sweater? Is the place where you live leaking heat through badly-fitting windows and uninsulated walls and roof?

IT'S AN ELECTRIC ELECTRIC-APPLIANCE POLISHER

If the TV is on, is someone actually watching it, or is it entertaining the furniture in an empty room? Unless you have a genuine disability, do you honestly need an electric toothbrush? carving knife? scissors?

Is the washing machine running for two t-shirts and a pair of socks? Is the drier flinging clothes about in a stream of hot air while the sun shines down on an empty washing line?

Finally, think on this. Save energy and you are not just saving the planet, you are saving yourself money. Or, possibly, you are saving someone else money. And they'll love you for that.

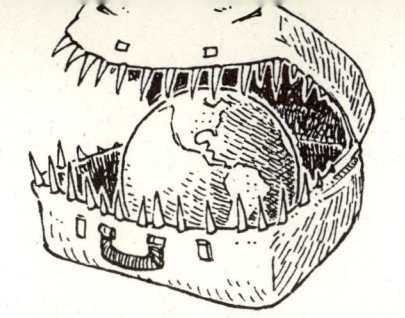

Chapter Sixteen

GET AWAY

Or: Should holiday brochures carry a planet-health warning?

If for some reason you wanted to destroy the planet by stealth, your best option would be to go on extravagant holidays all year round.

Most holiday brochures don't tell you this. Often, all they tell you is that you'll get good weather and a classy hotel with a private beach. They don't mention the people who used to farm the land on which the whacking great hotel now stands. Or the people who used to fish from the shore before the beach became private (not in order to look picturesque for photographs, but to catch lunch).

Few holiday-makers wish to know that, anyway. Holiday-time is time-out-of-life. Someone on holiday is a stranger living in a dream.

WRECKEM TOURS

WANT TO WRECK SOME OF THE MOST UNSPOILT PLACES ON EARTH?

WHY NOT GO ABROAD?
- DRIVE local people from traditional way of life
- FLY off the handle when they can't speak English
- SWIM in the pool that dries up the local water supply
- SAIL home in blissful ignorance of what happens to the waste you left behind

Nothing seems entirely real, so it isn't easy to believe that anything has real consequences.

"Your Holiday: A Chance To Get Away From It All" is a

terrific selling line (even though it overlooks the fact that most people seem to take it all with them, and then leave much of it behind when they come home again). However: "Your Holiday: A Chance To Turn Paradise Into A Cesspit" isn't likely to win an award from anybody's publicity department.

From the planet's point of view, tourism is an exceedingly new idea. Travel is different. People have always travelled – looking for food and water, exploring, trading, going on pilgrimages, making war – but tourism just for fun didn't really begin until the middle of the nineteenth century when Thomas Cook had his brainwave and invented package tours. Since then it has grown almost beyond belief, and the damage to the environment has been horrible – not least by modern hotels, in excitingly exotic locations, whose efficient plumbing reassures visitors.

Unsurprisingly, most visitors have other things on their minds than enquiring what happens to the sewage once it leaves the building. Equally unsurprisingly, the hotel doesn't post up this information in the lobby beside the dinner menu. So hardly anyone finds out that not only does no decent sewage treatment system exist, no one has plans to provide one, either.

And that is why mountain streams from Nepal to the Pyrenees are tainted, why beaches from the Philippines to the Mediterranean are polluted, why Bali's coral reefs and the shellfish in the Gulf of Thailand are suffering.

Up in the mountains and out in the game parks the clean air is being fogged up by pollution from charter aircraft and exhaust from cars and minibuses – more so when people keep their engines running for the sake of the air conditioning or heater while they admire the view.

It's tempting to say, "The world's a big place – what I do when I take a break isn't going to make a significant difference." That would almost certainly be true if it wasn't for the unfortunate fact that approximately 450 million other people are saying exactly the same thing.

Each year, 450 million tourists travel internationally, including the 100 million who go to the Mediterranean, the 50 million who head for the Alps and the 100,000 who go tribal trekking in Thailand. And 400 million annual visits are made to the National Parks of North America, putting almost intolerable pressure on plants and animals. (It's possible that the National Parks figure accounts for 200 million people who each went twice, but that doesn't really help.) Based on figures supplied by Tourism Concern

Part of the problem is that people expect luxury even when visiting very poor countries, regardless of what this does to the countryside, or what it takes from local people.

A visitor from another galaxy might well ask questions. Like – "If you can't manage without an *en suite*

> DAD, HAVE YOU SEEN MY HAIRDRYER?

> SURE DEAR, IT'S BEHIND THE CARPET SHAMPOOER

bathroom, imported bed linen and the kind of food you are used to – could you perhaps stay at home?"

"You're going solely for the hot weather? So how about buying a sunbed?"

"Why do you have to regard the local people either as a load of primitive sub-human dimwits or else as the superhuman guardians of ancient wisdom? Why (and this one could be easier to answer) do the local people regard the tourists either as greedy exploiters or rich benefactors? Can't you all make a huge leap of the imagination and see each other as people?"

Like so much else – it doesn't have to be like this. Tourism organised well brings in money and creates jobs. Numerous towns and villages all over the globe depend on it for their very survival. For them it would be a total disaster if it were to stop.

It can even act as a force for conservation. No one is going to dynamite a coral reef and feed the bits into a lime kiln if they can earn more by ferrying tourists through the shallows to admire it.

Also, it's fun.

But when it isn't organised well, almost all the money goes to the tour operators and to the people who fly in vast quantities of food because the visitors won't eat the local produce. Foreigners are imported to do all the decent jobs and the displaced farmers and other locals have to compete for careers as pool cleaners and bed makers. Perhaps most crucially of all, local people are left out at the planning stage which means they have no say at all in the way in which tourism is developed in their own area.

And conservation? In some of the more famous and popular ski resorts the removal of trees to build pistes and chair lifts has caused erosion and landslides – followed by the damage done by the construction of purpose-built resorts with their new roads and car parks and hotels.

The total length of Alpine ski-lifts would go round the Earth three times – the total length of roads and rail-track would go round ten times. Cross-country (or Nordic) ski-ing does less damage because it uses existing tracks and no ski lifts. Information supplied by Green Magazine *and Tourism Concern*

And now the weather is becoming more unpredictable, and the travel agent can no longer promise perfect conditions, technology is being installed in selected spots to siphon up millions of gallons of much-needed water and spew it out again as artificial snow.

If you have read this far, you may think you are being asked to compost your holiday brochures and spend all your free time cultivating the back garden. That would be nice, of course, but it isn't essential. Guilt-free holidays are possible.

You have to pay attention, though. Not everything that sounds innocent is.

What could be gentler than drifting above a game park in a balloon, what could be greener than trekking on foot through Nepal, what could be more peaceful than a golfing holiday?

Have you ever watched the reactions of animals – even domestic sheep and cattle – when a hot air balloon wheezes threateningly over their horizon? Environmentally friendly trekkers in Nepal, building their fires to cook and keep warm, each burn – in a single day – enough wood to supply a local family for a week. Forests are being lost to make space for trekkers' lodges, and to provide timber to build them and fuel their hot showers.

Wetlands have been drained, farmland destroyed and trees felled to create golf courses. Once the courses are laid out, water stocks are depleted so the grass on the fairways will be green enough to keep the balls rolling.

Spare a thought for holiday snaps. Disposable cameras are wasteful and button batteries and photographic fluids are toxic. Some photographic shops recycle the batteries, and some labs dispose of the toxic waste responsibly.

The important thing to remember is that tourism is a big money industry and money means power. So multinational tour operators, airlines and hotel chains have power and can make demands of holiday areas. They can bully and bribe people off their land to make way for new resorts. They can insist on lavish facilities. They can order the provision of snow, swimming pools, marinas, theme parks, speed boats, microlights and the rest, regardless of what it may mean to the water supply or the wildlife. They can dictate unreasonably low prices for locally made crafts. They can command regular performances of religious ceremonies and dances that should only take place on one special day of the year.

However, although they are powerful, they are not all-powerful. Since they are driven by a desire to make money, the people who really hold the power are the people whose money they want – the tourists – us. So if we refuse to use travel operators, airlines or hotels unless they can show that they are trying to avoid causing damage – and, better still, are actively repairing the damage they've already caused – they will shape-up. They will be forced to.

The obvious snag is that each big company operates as a single unified force, whereas tourists are a mixed and scattered bunch who mostly don't know each other and might prefer not to. So it's rather like trying to send a lot of miniature, unco-ordinated St Georges to tame large, strong and intelligent dragons. Not an encouraging image, until you remember there are only a few dragons and 450 million potential St Georges – and if the St Georges unite by joining a group (see Tourism Concern in Address List) a huge amount of damage-limitation becomes possible.

Some large hotel chains already minimise their waste and recycle the rest. Some tour operators already offer people green holidays. Some authorities already prevent over-development of resorts, and make sure that any acceptable development is undertaken by and for local people. Some operators will support local economies by training people for top jobs, by allowing the proper price to be paid for local pottery and other crafts, by encouraging visitors to try to understand the place they are visiting and not exploit it, and to enjoy the food of the region, supplied by local farmers and prepared by local cooks.

Look out for the green operators – but check they're as green as they claim. What is the point of having a sophisticated sewage disposal system if the hotel is built over an ancient burial ground (as in Hawaii), or the golf course and swimming pool use so much water that local people only have supplies for two hours a day (as in Thailand)?

Also, try to avoid tours that promise to take you to remote and unspoilt places. At the risk of sounding offensive, it has to be said that if you go, they may not remain unspoilt for long.

> Douglas Adams writing about Bali in *Last Chance to See...* (Pan Books, 1990): "When we told our guide that we didn't want to go to all the tourist places he took us instead to the places where they take tourists who say that they don't want to go to tourist places. These places are, of course, full of tourists ... it does highlight the irony that everything you go to see is changed by the very action of going to see it ..."

Chapter Seventeen
GET GREEN FINGERS

Or: Is this a side effect of squashing greenfly by hand?

Gardening can be a murderous affair. Encouraging things to grow seems to involve a lot of killing. Sometimes more than intended. Slugs which eat slug pellets usually die, as planned. However, birds and hedgehogs may eat slugs which have recently eaten slug pellets, and eventually the build-up of poison can kill them, too. Not part of the plan. Other garden chemicals, especially pesticides and weedkillers, do even more damage, and do it more rapidly.

Because pesticides are marketed in bright and cheery packages in the friendly local garden centre, they seem much safer than they actually are. Logically, though, it's unlikely that anything which poisons large groups of invertebrates is going to be especially beneficial to anything else that lives. Many garden chemicals should be used with exaggerated caution, if at all, and one – paraquat – has

> "Every year, dogs, cats, hedgehogs, and many, many beneficial insects are killed by garden chemicals used in the wrong place, at the wrong time." The Soil Association

no known antidote. (Paraquat is actually banned in several countries, but, oddly, not in the UK.) The flies, mites, bugs, grubs and slugs that eat garden plants, and the self-sown so-called weeds that crowd the plants out and choke them, are very real, though, and clearly some sort of action has to be taken.

There are acceptable (pump-action) bug-sprays, but there are also other methods – including leaving out saucers of beer for slugs to drown in, and pulling weeds and squashing greenfly by hand.

One thoroughly researched and generally successful method is companion planting. This can take various forms.

It can mean, for example, putting nasturtiums next to runner beans so that blackfly, which, on the whole, prefer nasturtiums, will congregate on those and leave the beans clear. This doesn't work if what you wanted was to grow competition-standard nasturtiums.

It can mean planting something strong-smelling – garlic or spring onion – between other plants to deter insects.

It can mean putting together two kinds of plants which are known to flourish better together than apart. (In some cases, research has discovered a complementary chemical reaction between the good companions – in other cases, no one knows why it works, but observation over the generations has shown that it does.) Healthy, strong plants can survive a certain amount of insect attack without much difficulty.

Another possibility is encouraging natural predators. Some insect larvae can endanger aphid populations quite nicely if there are enough of them. Star performers are the young of ladybirds, lacewings (which look slightly like huge greenfly, but aren't) and some types of hoverfly.

Insect-eating birds are useful, and so are snail-eating thrushes, and hedgehogs who work through an extensive menu of slugs, grubs and beetles.

If the predators are too dim to spot the food opportunities and move in of their own accord, there are ways of encouraging them. Some of the predatory insects can actually be bought and released in the garden as required. So can various types of nematode – microscopic parasitic worms, sold in tiny packs in multiples of five million. Nematodes could be the stuff of nightmares, but are advertised as harmless (except to their specific prey) by trustworthy organisations and, in any case, they exist naturally in most soils. There's one kind which eats vine weevil larvae before the vine weevil larvae can eat the plant-roots away. Others with different but equally useful appetites are currently being inspected for commercial use.

(Is it fair to attack vine weevil grubs in this way? Are we prejudiced against them because they are not attractive, because they don't have faces, or fur? Do we dislike them for flimsy reasons, like – not only do they not have fur, they're so damp and pale they look as though they're inside out? Is there any good reason why they shouldn't be allowed to eat most of the roots of the plant and then develop, as nature intended, into weevils, which will climb up the stems and eat the leaves and flowers? Thus finishing off the plant completely. This is a moral dilemma which each person must confront alone. Or, if you take my advice, in the company of five million parasitic worms.)

If you would rather predatory larvae arrived of their own volition, try planting things the adults like. For example, hoverflies feed on nectar and are particularly partial to buddleia – which also appeals to butterflies. In fact, it's possible that buddleia is the most famous environmentally friendly plant of them all, but it can grow quite large and may not be entirely suitable for tiny gardens.

There are numerous other plants which are the chosen food of glamorous or useful insects. But plants have their own particular requirements, and gardens differ – size, type of soil, amount of sunlight, direction and degree of prevailing wind, etc. What will flourish in one plot may wither in another. If you're unsure, then contact WATCH (see Address List). They can put you in touch with your local Wildlife Trust who will know what works best in the area. The Soil Association (companion-planting a speciality) and The Henry Doubleday Research Association (all aspects of organic gardening) publish invaluable leaflets and books – see Address List.

The best way to get birds into the garden is to provide safe places to nest and hide, a regular supply of water, and food in winter. You can also grow plants whose seeds and berries appeal, like sunflowers, cotoneaster and pyracantha. The Royal Society for the Protection of Birds (see Address List) publishes a useful leaflet called 'Planting Gardens for Birds', if you really want to get into it properly.

Hedgehogs are keen on privacy and water, too. A dish of water will do. A pond would be nice (you might get frogs as well) but don't dig something with steep sides. Hedgehogs like to swim but appreciate being able to get out again afterwards.

The Hedgehog Preservation Society (see Address List) publish a leaflet called 'How To Make a Wildlife Garden', and various others on the specific requirements of garden-hogs and the best ways of persuading one to include your place on its rounds.

The HPS also has a network of carers all over the country who look after injured or sick hedgehogs. Anyone with a safe, walled, pesticide-free garden can apply to take on a blind hedgehog, or perhaps an amputee. But you will be inspected first, and there is a waiting list (of safe havens, not of wounded hedgehogs).

The one snag about hedgehogs is that they eat worms, which are good for the garden, but their mixed diet means they don't de-worm too seriously.

Although worms look as though they eat earth, they actually eat the organic matter that it contains. They aerate the soil and their casts can be good fertiliser. So rich is the manure produced by mealworms (which are farmed as fishing bait) that it is sold commercially under the name of Wormi Doo. (Say what you like about the title, the Soil Association confirms that it's good stuff.) There is also a great vogue for setting up a wormery in the garden to produce worm-crap on site. Among the things you can feed to the wormery are torn up newspapers and kitchen waste, so you can recycle while you revitalise. (The HDRA will advise.)

Having thought about what you might attract to the garden, spare a thought for what you might get rid of. Like grass. In a dry summer, lawn sprinklers can account for about a third of all domestic water used. In the US, and now also in Canada and Australia, more and more garden designers are using drought-tolerant ground cover plants to replace lawns with their serious drink problems.

> "Some garden sprinklers can spray out up to 264 gallons an hour – about the amount a family of four would get through in two days."

> "A lawnmower driven by a petrol engine produces as much hydrocarbon in one hour as a car driven 80km."
> *New Scientist*, (29 August 1992)

It might be nice if garden machinery could go too.

Lawnmowers and strimmers – especially strimmers – probably account for more hedgehog deaths and injuries than road accidents do. They are especially lethal in late spring and early summer – the strimmers usual hunting season – when pregnant hedgehogs are making their nests in exactly the places where the strimmer strims. Frogs, low-built bird nests, voles, young children, small domestic animals and the feet of the strimmer-operative are also at risk. Neat edges and carnage

fig I — lawnmower

fig II — lawnmower

are what you get with a strimmer. Whiskery edges and wildlife seem infinitely preferable.

And then there's peat. Peat in one form or another – straight, mixed or moulded into pots – has been sold in garden centres for years. Some people are so accustomed to using it that they do it without thinking. The green-fingered gardeners of Britain are directly responsible for about half the losses suffered by peat bogs – which are rich wildlife habitats and also, as it happens, quite useful for storing water and eking it out as streams.

Pressure from environmental groups is beginning to make a difference and alternatives are appearing. The Soil Association and the HDRA have advice on this, and the RSPB and FoE publish leaflets on peat-free gardening. Alternatives for mulches (which are spread between plants, or on empty beds awaiting plants, to keep down weeds and stop the soil drying out) include leaf mould, home-made compost, bark, coconut shell, or coir (coconut hair). Sheets of plastic work well, too, and so do sheets of newspaper.

Newspaper is good raw material for making substitute peat-pots. (Peat pots are the ones you can grow seeds in and then plant out as they are, without disturbing the seedling roots.) Shredded up wet paper moulded round a small plant pot and lifted off when dry works quite well – given that the thing is supposed to rot down anyway once it gets into the earth.

It's tougher when it comes to buying potting compost for window boxes or tubs. It can be hard to find peat-free versions – even the ones made up of mixtures of manure, coir, bark and loam often have about 25% peat in them. You can only do your best – which should include asking the garden centre to find a supplier of genuinely peat-free stuff. Or get on to Chase Organics (see Address List) who provide peat-free compost by mail order.

Having got your garden pesticide-pest-peat-and-power-appliance free, you might consider feeding and watering it.

If you live in the country, it

shouldn't be hard to get hold of manure (in a manner of speaking!) In urban areas it's not so easy.

Natural fertilisers may be available from the local garden centre (read the small print), and are certainly available from Chase Organics among other places, but the serious gardener-recycler will have a compost heap. Much has been written on this subject – what can go on the heap, when to fork it over, how best to speed up the natural rotting down process, when to spread it on or dig it into the earth. Don't let all the advice deter. Start by throwing the kitchen waste into a discreet corner – and then you'll be forced to decide what to do next.

In dry summers, when hose-pipe bans weigh heavily, try recycling once-used household water on to the garden. It is possible to set up some practical plumbing arrangements which will pump or siphon water out of the bath or sink, but if you can't manage any of those, bail. The water can be collected in a rain-butt. Don't use water that is polluted with undesirables – bath salts and oils, heavy duty household cleaners, etc. Washing up water is fine and water that has been used to wash vegetables is perfect.

Naturally, there should be a rainbutt in place to catch the run-off from the roof as well. (If yours is an old roof, find out if there's any lead up there. Lead contamination in the garden could be a problem – especially if you're growing things to eat.)

If you find you've conserved more water than you need, throw it away and start again. Left to get stagnant it will breed unpleasant primitive life forms.

Not everybody has a garden, but it's possible to practise organic cultivation in a window box or in a pot-garden indoors. If that seems limiting, an alternative is to get involved with a local Community Garden or City Farm (check with The National Federation of City Farms and Community Gardens, see Address List). If there isn't one already, is there any chance of forming a group and starting one? (Take a lot of advice first, though, it isn't as easy at it may sound.)

If none of that is possible, the local Wildlife Trust (see above) probably needs volunteers to help carry out various kinds of practical conservation work on nature reserves, ponds, streams, woodlands and so on. Needless to say, it's an extremely bad idea to launch a solo campaign in any of these areas. It's crucial to work with a recognised group which knows what it's about. Otherwise you risk doing more harm than good – not to mention encountering the neighbourhood psychopath in some lonely spot.

Finally – plant a tree – or raise the money so somebody else can.

LOOK AT THAT LITTLE TREE... I THINK I'LL TAKE THAT HOME SO THE KIDS CAN PLANT IT

Chapter Eighteen

GET THIS!

Or: Is this label lying to me?

A photograph of a red-kneed tarantula is considerably less appealing than a photograph of a week-old kitten – to most people, anyway. Yet they are about the same size and equally furry. And since we're talking still pictures here, neither of them is engaging in menacing or cute behaviour.

The difference is in packaging and association. Four legs, pointy ears and large eyes are acceptable; also kittens are known to be affectionate, playful and all-round endearing. Eight legs, no perceivable eyes or ears and hairy mandibles are unacceptable; and few people have ever taken the trouble to discover whether or not tarantulas are faithful, loving and frolicsome.

Packaging uses the obvious fact that some things are more attractive than others – but it uses it in so many different ways that the consumer often responds favourably without in the least knowing why. Packaging designers have always tried to give the message: 'this product is the best.' Now that more and more people are becoming concerned about pollution, the message has been extended. What they are trying to say now is: 'this product is the best *and* the greenest.' If you

139

would prefer to choose things because of what they really offer, not because of what they seem to offer, then you need to see past these marketing ploys. (But don't become totally cynical. Just occasionally, something which is marketed as being green and nourishing actually is.)

Everything about a packet, jar, bottle or other container is designed to sell the product. Shape and texture are carefully considered. Colour plays a vital role. Blue implies a product is hygenic. Green indicates it is environmentally friendly. Brown suggests it is earthy, traditional, and better for you and the planet than a product packaged in bright red.

Pictures are crucial. Illustrations of wheat, flowers, herbs and green fields add to the wholesome image. So do illustrations of healthy people (or animals) with bright eyes, laughing mouths revealing perfect teeth, and shining hair.

Great care goes into the choice of typeface, size of print and positioning of the text. The design of the top, bottom, sides and back of a package are given as much attention as the design of the front – no one can be certain which bit of it the shopper will see first.

And then there are the words themselves.

At worst, they lie.

Two major DIY suppliers have stuck notices on their stocks of tropical hardwood frames and veneers which read: 'Manufactured From

Sustainable Timber' and 'Harvested In Such A Way As To Safeguard The Ecological Balance', when this was blatantly untrue. One even pretended to have the support of Friends of the Earth.

Doubtless there are honest DIY stockists who are making truthful statements about the acceptability of their timber, but the sad fact is that you can't believe anyone. Sometimes claims are made which are meaningless, confusing or hugely exaggerated.

FoE gave their 1989 Green Con of the Year Award to a motor manufacturer (who shall remain nameless – why should they get free advertising!). They had claimed their newest model was 'ozone-friendly' because it could run on unleaded petrol – neatly overlooking the fact that lead has no effect on the ozone layer.

Packaging is advertising (technical term: brand imaging) and the ISBA (Incorporated Society of British Advertisers) aims 'to ensure that British advertising is legal, honest, decent and truthful . . .'

Among others who keep a close eye on all kinds of advertising are The Advertising Standards Commission, the ITV Association, the Independent Television Commission, the Radio Authority, the Department of Trade and Industry, the Consumers' Association, all the environmental pressure groups – and the industry itself. Most complaints about labelling claims are made by companies against their competitors! But by the time an untruthful claim has been banned it has already beguiled numerous shoppers into believing it.

Here is an alphabet of statements to watch out for:

Biodegradable. Something which is easily broken down by bacterial organisms and accepted back into earth or water without causing damage. Claims are usually true but sometimes overstated. For example, the main cleaning agents in detergents, surfactants, must, by law, be at least 80% biodegradable within 19 days, so to claim a washing powder is biodegradable is to overstate the case. It is possible that surfactants made from vegetable oils rather than petrochemicals biodegrade more rapidly.

Biological. Soap powders which claim to be 'biological' contain enzymes which digest protein and starch and help break down stains. Enzymes are not thought to be pollutants but can cause skin reactions in some people.

Caffeine-free. Caffeine – found in tea leaves and coffee beans among other places – is a heart stimulant. Too much can make people jumpy and nervous. BUT – 'caffeine-free' has been spotted on a can of soup. Soup never does contain caffeine!

Care or Caring. These words are open to various interpretations. In labelling or advertising they are almost always meaningless.

Chlorine-free. Many pulp products, including sanitary towels and disposable nappies, offer a chlorine-free option. Some products are now oxygen bleached (considered a less environmentally-damaging process) or use hydrogen peroxide.

Cruelty-free or Not tested on animals. The product itself may not have been tested on animals, but its component parts may have been. According to the RSPCA, every ingredient, natural or synthetic, is likely to have been tested on animals at some point in the past. However, as nothing can be done about the past, the best bet is to try to prevent present and future testing. Companies will usually state how long their ingredients have been cruelty-free. For example, the Body Shop and Body Reform refuse to use a substance that has been tested on animals in the last five years, while Beauty without Cruelty insists on ten years. (Worryingly, it is a rolling five or ten years.)

Decaffeinated. See Caffeine-free, above. There are various methods of decaffeinating coffee – at least one involves the use of chemicals which may be more unpleasant than the caffeine they are removing.

Dolphin friendly (tuna). The Whale and Dolphin Conservation Society says the industry is 'moving in the right direction' but that no one currently trading in tuna in this country can be completely confident that the tuna being bought, or the canneries being dealt with, are in fact dolphin friendly. However, some companies are quite certain that their tuna is caught by rod and line, not by the nets which trap and drown dolphins and whales, and will say so on the label. Many are going to great lengths to be sure their claims are truthful – Heinz, for instance, gets its fish from Ecuador where the government has a 'no dolphin deaths' policy, and where the Inter-American Tropical Tuna Commission places independent inspectors on every boat.

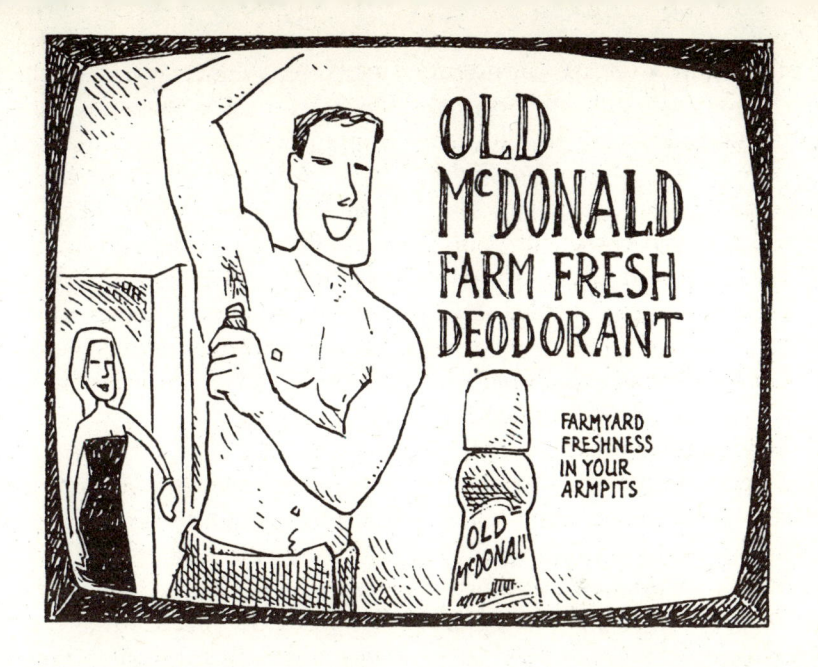

Environmentally friendly. This is unlikely to be true of the entire product and all its packaging. A misleading term which shouldn't be used.

Farm fresh. Meaningless; what kind of farm – intensive – battery – organic? Fresh when?

Farmhouse. See above.

Flavoured versus Flavour. If

a product is described as 'blackcurrant' or 'blackcurrant flavoured', most or all of the taste must come from real blackcurrants. However, something described as 'blackcurrant flavour' need never have been within a mile of a blackcurrant; the flavouring is probably synthetic.

Free range. Free range chickens, whether for laying or eating or both, must have daytime access to runs where they can scratch about in the normal way. They must also have indoor space in which to perch and rest at night. Because European producers have different standards, there are currently three sub-definitions – 1, Free Range, 2, Traditional Free Range and 3, Free-Range, Total Freedom. The differences are in the amount of indoor and outdoor space available to each hen (1 having the least and 3 the most). Labelling is not always clear on this, but chickens kept in any of these three ways are all living reasonably natural lives. Eggs labelled Farm Fresh or Country Fresh come from intensive, or 'battery' farms. Barn eggs are from hens kept in 'percheries' which sometimes pack in 25 birds to the square metre. Although they are not individually caged, and do have perches to fly up to, each bird may actually have less floor space than it would have in a battery cage, and there is rarely enough room for all the birds to be on the ground at once or for all to roost at once, so their options are limited. Better to buy Barn eggs than eggs from battery-farmed hens, but better still to look for Free Range – and if you can find 'Free Range, Total Freedom', go for it.

Fresh. Makes sense if it is used to mean 'not frozen'. Does not make sense if it is supposed to mean 'not stale'. As the word won't obliterate itself on an agreed date, a 30-year-old-pack will still claim freshness.

Friendlier or Greener. Than what? Acceptable only where a genuine improvement, in environmental terms, can be demonstrated. In other words, somewhere on the package there should be a clear explanation of why the greener/friendlier claim is being made. If there isn't one – the words probably mean nothing.

Good for you. Meaningless. You will notice that the product usually doesn't tell you in what way it is good for you. A certain chocolate product which says it 'contains the goodness of full cream milk' has the same amount of fat, calories and calcium as any other chocolate and is just as bad for teeth.

Greener – see Friendlier.

High Fibre. Fibre combines with water in the bowel and eases the passage of digestible food through the intestine. Claims that it can reduce blood cholesterol are not proven. Some breakfast cereals that make a big performance about being extra high in fibre keep rather quiet about the fact that they are also extra high in salt and sugar. EU proposals suggest that the term should only be used if there is more than 6g per 100g in solid or liquid foods.

Home-cooked. Meaningless – whose home?

Healthy – see Good For You.

Kind or Kinder. As meaningless as Caring (above), unless the label states that the product contains an ingredient that counteracts the harshness of the detergent/shampoo etc – or that it contains less of a specific harsh ingredient than it used to.

Life-enhancing. Some bottled waters claim to 'participate in the maintenance of your fitness'. All water does this. Others to 'cleanse away impurities'; they don't explain what they mean by this. The manufacturers of a mixed fruit drink who claim the drink has special properties have accepted that this statement doesn't mean much, and are changing it.

Light (or lite, lighter, lightly). A recent marketing word. Something labelled 'light' may have less fat or sugar but much the same amount of calories. For example, 'light' syrup in tinned fruit has a thinner consistency but even more calories than ordinary syrup. It can also be used to mean light in colour or light in apparent weight, without necessarily meaning 'less fattening'.

Low or Lower. Read the rest of the labelling. 'Low fat' or 'low sugar' are often claimed for a product which would carry little fat or sugar anyway. Under new EU regulations (which are just coming into force twelve years after the first guidelines were drawn up), foods can only make the following claims: low calorie if they have less than 50kcals per 100g; low fat if they have less than 5g per 100g; low in saturates if they have less than 3g per 100g and less than 15% energy from saturates; low sugar if they have less than 5g per 100g; low sodium or low salt if they have less than 120mg sodium per 100g; low cholesterol if they have less than 20mg per 100g, plus meeting conditions for low saturates claim.

Foods which are not allowed to claim, for example, 'low fat', may well be allowed to claim 'reduced fat'. These regulations still need more work because they don't take into account the different sizes of average servings of different foods. *WHICH?* points out that "some tinned spaghetti has less than 5g of sugar per 100g, so it could carry a 'low sugar' claim, but a typical serving is about 200g, and 10g is quite a hefty chunk of sugar." And why in the world does anyone put sugar into canned spaghetti in the first place? Presumably because we've all got so used to things tasting sweet that we even tolerate sugar in toothpaste!

For liquids the figures per 100ml are: low calorie, less than 25kcals; low fat, less than 2.5g; low saturates, less than 1.5g and less than 15% energy from saturates; low sugar, less than 2.5g; low sodium or low salt, less than 60 mg sodium; low cholesterol, less than 10mg plus meeting conditions for low saturates claim.

Natural. By implication this means 'made by nature' (note that nature also made swamp fever and venomous snakes!). But almost everything in the shops has experienced human interference – and most packaged foodstuffs contain preservatives at the very least. Occasionally, something marketed as 'natural' proudly lists the additives it does NOT contain – like the bottled water which was labelled 'Additive free and no cholesterol'. What additives would you put in water, and how could it possibly contain cholesterol?

No nitrates. This is an interesting one which can often appear on bathroom cleaners. It's true enough, but on the other hand there is no such thing as a UK bathroom cleaner that DOES contain nitrates.

Organic. Should only be used in the actual name of the product if at least 95% of the ingredients are organic. May appear in the list of ingredients (but not in the name) if between half and 95% of the ingredients are organic. Must not appear anywhere on the pack if less than half the ingredients are organic.

All UK organic food producers, processors and importers are registered (directly or through an approved body) with the UK Register of Organic Food Standards. UKROFS has strict rules on the use of fertilisers, additives, pest control, packaging and on the protection of wildlife habitats. There are five bodies in the UK currently approved and their symbols appear on food and drink labelling – The Soil Association, The Bio-Dynamic Agricultural Association, The Organic Farmers and Growers Ltd (OFG), the Scottish Organic Producers Association (SOPA) and the Organic Food Federation.

Ozone friendly or **Ozone safe.** Under guidelines produced by the professional advertising associations and the DTI, this should only be used for products which once contained some ozone-layer-damaging chemicals but no longer do.

FoE presented their 1991 'So What' Award to a bottle of shampoo which was labelled 'Ozone friendly', even though there is no such thing as Ozone unfriendly shampoo.

Phosphate-free. On the

labelling of some washing-up liquids – implying that their rivals do contain phosphates. But according to *WHICH?*, no UK washing-up liquids do contain phosphates. (See No nitrates, above.) Some detergents do contain phosphates, so 'phosphate-free' on washing powder or liquid should be a valid claim.

Preventing disease. Medicines are the only products allowed to claim they prevent disease. If you see the claim on a food label, complain.

Pure. 'Pure' butter means just that. But what is pure soap? Soap is made from many ingredients, often including chemicals, animal fats and stearic acid, a solid fat. Pure and simple are words which sound nice but don't necessarily mean anything.

Rich in . . . (usually followed by the name of a vitamin or trace mineral). But if a carton of orange juice claims to be 'Rich in Vitamin C' it is simply using what is already in the juice as a selling point. Under proposed EU regulations, any foods or drinks claiming to be 'rich in' anything must contain more than 30% of the daily recommended requirement per 100g.

Source of . . . (vitamins, fibre or whatnot). At the moment there are no legal definitions and although the food must contain whatever it claims to be a source of, the amount isn't specified.

Traditional. Meaningless term – used on packaging to indicate 'wholesome' (whatever that means).

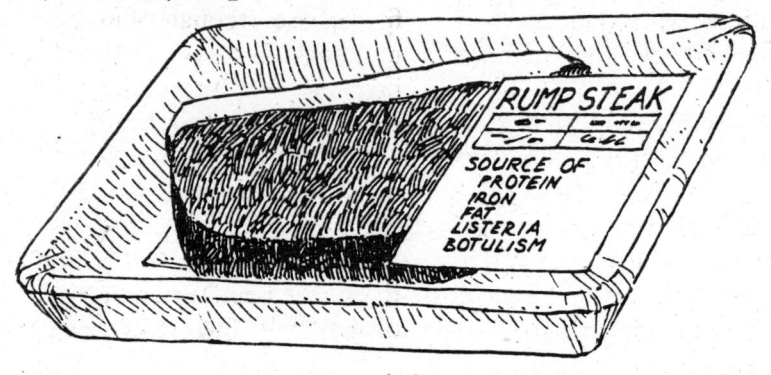

E Numbers. Often, food labelling does give genuine information. For example, it must, by law, list all additives – the famous E numbers.

Some people automatically avoid any product which contains additives, but not all E numbered additives are bad for you. E160a is an orangey-red colouring which is mostly extracted from carrots. E322, used as an emulsifier to stop fat separating (in ice cream, for instance) is lecithin which comes from soya beans. E300 is ascorbic acid, otherwise known as Vitamin C, and positively beneficial. E406 is a gelling agent made from extract of seaweed.

The most disagreeable of them are only present in small quantities. Even if you eat something which contains E220 (sulphur dioxide, bad for anyone with asthma or troubles with their liver or kidneys), E102 (the infamous tartrazine, blamed for hyperactivity in children), or E123 (the purplish-red Amaranth which is now banned in several European countries) you will not be getting much. Unless you have a specific allergy, or some other physical problem, small amounts are unlikely to do any harm. However, if you eat a lot of foods which all contain the same additive, you could be raising the dose rather high.

Certain additives are banned by law from foods made especially for babies and small children. This suggests they may not be all that good for the rest of us. They are: all the artificial sweeteners; all the colourings (except for three orangey-yellow ones, E101 and E101a, which are B-complex vitamins, and E160a which is Beta-Carotene); the preservatives E250 and E251, which are sodium nitrite and sodium nitrate; the antioxidants E310, E311, E312, E320, E321; and the flavour enhancers E621, E622, E623, E627, E631 and E635.

As a general guide, it's useful to know that the E means the EU passed the additive as fit for use (though some E numbers have since been banned in many individual countries). A number without an E in front means the Union does not find it acceptable, but the country of origin has decided that it is. All additives have been tested individually, but few tests have been run to see if some gangs of additives are more noxious than others.

E numbers beginning with E1 are colourings. Those beginning with E2 are preservatives. E3s are mostly antioxidants (to stop fats from going rancid and colours from fading) and emulsifiers. E4s are thickeners, stabilisers and sometimes sweeteners. E5s are mainly to improve texture (to stop things going into lumps) and also sometimes to improve flavour.

E6s are all flavour enhancers. The most widely used flavour enhancer is E621, which is monosodium glutamate (banned for babies, see above). It's made from fermented soya beans and is thought to cause temporary dizziness and headaches in some people.

E120, cochineal, a red colouring made from coccus cacti, a scale insect which feeds on cactus and prickly pear, is banned in Spain and Norway, and is not acceptable to strict vegetarians.

If you're interested or concerned, buy one of the dictionaries (*E for Additives*, for example) which will tell you exactly what each one is, what it is supposed to do for the food, and what it might do to you by mistake.

And finally, the EU has introduced a special logo awarded to products which meet certain environmental standards. But the whole process has turned out to be far more complicated than anyone expected, and many environmentalists are afraid that the standards have been set too low and are too vague.

As a for instance – the committee was so daunted at the complexity of the whole issue of whether a product, or any part of it, had or had not been tested on animals that they dropped the whole thing. This means that a cosmetic which is regularly tested on animals could bear the logo if it meets certain other requirements.

It is going to take a lot of lobbying, pushing, complaints and encouragement to get a decent Ecolabelling system going. But as you will realise, if you have read this far, it is urgently needed. (It would also help if the British Government kept its promise to amend the Trade Descriptions Act to outlaw misleading green claims.)

> "Giving labels to disposable products, testing products on animals, using industry data without cross-checking and allowing standards to be set at embarrassingly low levels, in the end offers little help to the consumer – and even less to our polluted planet." Bernadette Vallely, Director of the Women's Environmental Network, writing in *The Independent* (1 June 1993)

Chapter Nineteen

WHAT THE STARS SAY

Or: How green is your sign?

Those who believe in astrology will tell you that it's no use studying your sun sign on its own. To cast an accurate horoscope you need to know the positions of all of the planets in all of the houses at the exact moment of your entry into the world. What this means, of course, is that when you look up your sun-sign in the green zodiac which follows, you need not pay any attention to what you read!

Aries (22 March to 20 April) The ram. A cardinal fire sign, ruled by the energetic and sometimes war-like planet Mars. At best – enterprising, brave and adventurous. At worst – impatient, argumentative and rude. A natural pioneer, eager to be first to try out new green products, but easily bored by fiddly details – like reading the small print on the pack.

The part of the body governed by Aries is the head (the word 'headstrong' might have been created for these people) and they tend to suffer from headaches and sunstroke so their main area of interest is likely to be the damage to the ozone layer.

(Aries falls in love quickly and dramatically and is passionate and enthusiastic – though not necessarily particularly tactful.)

Taurus (21 April to 21 May)
The bull (but not a raging bull, more of a peaceful ox). A fixed earth sign ruled by Venus. At best – practical, patient and kind. At worst – stubborn, stodgy and self-indulgent.

Taureans believe in conserving the Earth's resources and you'd expect them to be especially concerned about the destruction of the rainforests. A green Taurus would be a steady and reliable friend to the Earth. However, Taureans like their home comforts and an ungreen bull might surround itself with planet-damaging luxuries – comfortable mahogany lavatory seats, warm leopard skin rugs, and numerous labour-saving devices.

(Taurus falls in love slowly, even lazily, but once in love, stays there. Affectionate, warm – and possessive.)

Gemini (22 May to 22 June)
The twins. A mutable air sign, ruled by Mercury, smallest and fastest-moving of the planets. At best – intelligent, versatile and witty. At worst – unreliable, devious, gossipy and restless.

Geminis are very aware of their environment and are great communicators (and often vegetarians). An environmentally aware Gemini can be relied on to understand the issues and to explain them in a clear and lively way to a wide audience. However, a Gemini who is not functioning well is generally too impatient to read beyond the headlines. These are the people who confuse everyone by flinging around all sorts of disjointed and inaccurate bits of information.

(Gemini prefers flirting to falling in love, and can be fickle. Use your intelligence to keep a Gemini interested – and never ask for reassurance.)

Cancer (23 June to 22 July)
The crab (or, some say, the crayfish). A cardinal water sign ruled by the moon. At best – sympathetic, imaginative and protective. At worst – moody, manipulative and self-pitying. Often have crab-like characteristics – a tough exterior and a soft heart, the ability to pinch if cornered, a tendency to approach problems cautiously, not to mention sideways. The sign of Cancer governs the primal waters so you would expect a Cancerian to take action on the pollution of springs, streams and rivers. They are also nurturers, good with plants, though inclined to over-water. A Cancerian will never waste water or pour anything evil down the sink – but might, like Taurus, buy too many unsuitable home improvements or, like Pisces, subside uselessly into washy depression.

(Cancer in love is romantic – and reluctant to let go even when the relationship is over. Home and emotional security are important to Cancer.)

Leo (23 July to 23 August)
The lion. A fixed fire sign, ruled by the sun. Since the sun is a vast nuclear reactor and our primary source of light and heat, so Leos should be concerned about the creation and conservation of energy.

At best enthusiastic, generous and warm. At worst conceited, rather pushy and patronising. The typical Leo likes to be top lion, surrounded not just by comfort, but by showy luxury. An unenlightened Leo is a fat cat, lusting after huge petrol-hungry cars and environment-depleting consumables in extravagant quantities. The green Leo, though, will want to be the best green on the block – in town – in the universe. As an instinctive leader, a green Leo will encourage others to follow.

(Leo in love is wholehearted and faithful – but hates to be tied down too soon. Like most cats, Leos believe in open doors.)

Virgo (24 August to 23 September)
The virgin, holding a sheaf of corn, which suggests she's an earth goddess. A mutable earth sign ruled by Mercury (who also rules Gemini). Virgo's area of concern would be pollution of the earth itself, by the burying of toxic waste or the use of chemicals on farmland. At best – intelligent, efficient, keen to serve the community. At worst – critical and pedantic.

Cleanliness is very important to a Virgo and the ungreen sort will be heavy on the biological washing powders, caustic cleaners and ferocious disinfectants and will have an overstocked bathroom shelf. Once alerted to the problems, though, there is no sign more hard-working, and Virgo's efficiency and attention to detail will be invaluable.

(Virgo in love is conventional, cautious and good-humoured. You'll lose a Virgo if you're sloppy or untidy – and you won't attract one in the first place unless your personal hygiene is beyond reproach.)

Libra (24 September to 23 October)
The scales. A cardinal air sign ruled by Venus (which also rules Taurus). At best – charming, optimistic and peace-loving. At worst – indecisive, lazy, lacking in self-confidence.

Libra is a born diplomat with a strong sense of justice, the ideal person to negotiate with the representatives of governments, businesses and chemical companies – and anyone else who should be tactfully persuaded to act on behalf of the planet. Libra's main aim in life is to see that everything remains balanced, in a state of elegant equilibrium, which means they are instinctively green. But the danger here is that someone so excessively fair-minded could be persuaded to see the polluters' point of view.

(Libra in love is nearly as romantic as Cancer – but as keen for an intelligent partner as Gemini. To keep Libra happy make sure that everything is harmonious.)

Scorpio (24 October to 22 November)
The Scorpion. A fixed water sign ruled either by Mars (who also rules Aries) or else, so some say, by the small and remote Pluto. An intense and dramatic sign, powerful and mysterious, secretive but with a strong desire to uncover the secrets of others. At best – imaginative and intuitive with a sharp analytical mind. At worst – destructive (sometimes self-destructive), vindictive and cruel.

As this sign is linked with destruction and regeneration, Scorpio's main area of concern should be rubbish disposal and recycling. The green Scorpio will find this work intriguing and challenging and will have the energy to achieve great things – unless it all goes horribly wrong in which case an un-green Scorpion could become a vandal, a litter-lout, an all-round destroyer.

(Scorpio in love is perceptive, passionate, sexy and jealous. You can break off the relationship, if you want to, but never two-time a Scorpio.)

Sagittarius (23 November to 22 December)
The Archer – a centaur with a bow and arrow. A mutable fire sign ruled by Jupiter. Sagittarians are ambitious and adventurous, eager to travel and explore. At best – idealistic, open-minded and cheerful. At worst – extravagant, boastful and restless.

For obvious reasons, Sagittarians have a special affinity with horses – but they also care about other animals, especially land animals, and are likely to concern themselves with wildlife conservation. A green Sagittarian would go to almost any lengths to rescue an animal – an un-green Sagittarian might become a hunter or poacher.

(Sagittarius in love is as conventional as Virgo, as sincere as Taurus, but needs as much freedom as fiery Leo or airy Gemini.)

Capricorn (23 December to 19 January)

The goat with the fish's tail. A cardinal earth sign ruled by the huge planet Saturn with its many rings. The typical Capricorn is disciplined, prudent, methodical, and often rather serious. At best practical, responsible and conscientious. At worst cold, stingy and unfeeling.

A green Capricorn is likely to have the patience – and the scientific turn of mind – to work out solutions to the problems of acid rain and the greenhouse effect. If the goat is not green, though, it is capable of being too pessimistic and downright selfish to care.

(Capricorn is very cautious about falling in love, faithful once it happens, but not at all demonstrative. Never be frivolous around Capricorns, you'll only alarm them.)

Aquarius January to 19 February)

The water carrier. A fixed air sign ruled by Saturn (like Capricorn) or, some say, by Uranus. At best idealistic, broad-minded and artistic. At worst rebellious, untrustworthy and erratic.

Aquarians are reformers who take a wide view of things – more interested in the troubles of the world than of their own family. They believe in equality, justice and human rights – which suggests they are likely to be concerned with the problems of the Third World (their interest in photography and electronic communications could lead them to become documentary-makers). They are also quite eccentric. This means that while the green Aquarian is coming up with new and wholly beneficial ideas, the ungreen version is doing untold damage by seeking out unusual holidays in previously unspoilt places.

(Aquarians in love are quite romantic but can be perverse and changeable. They are drawn to genuinely unconventional people – but it's no use pretending, you'll be seen through at once.)

Pisces (20 February to 21 March)

The fishes. A mutable water sign ruled by Jupiter (like Sagittarius) and also by the mystical Neptune. The typical Pisces is sensitive, unworldly, sometimes psychic. At best kind, creative and artistic. At worst temperamental, gullible and vague.

Pisces is horrified by suffering and would join Aquarius and Sagittarius in caring for deprived people or animals. However, the power of Neptune in this sign means that oceans, and all that is in them, are the principal areas of concern. Pisces would like to stop oceanic pollution and save the whale. Dreamy Pisces could easily be completely unaware of environmental problems – but even an un-green Pisces is unlikely actually to damage the planet. A green Pisces will be self-sacrificing for the sake of the cause – but could go completely to pieces if shown too many tragic disasters.

(Pisces in love is emotional, gentle, generous and needs protection. And you'll have to do all the practical stuff.)

Chapter Twenty
WHAT ARE WE DOING?

Or: How green is the team?

It's extraordinarily annoying to be given advice – especially inconvenient advice – by people you strongly suspect are not following it themselves.

So we decided to be honest.

The Writer (Judy Allen):
I've hardly ever used aerosols – none at all for at least ten years – with one exception – my asthma-inhaler uses CFCs and until there is a substitute I can't give it up (I'm addicted to breathing). Also I have a non-green fridge, and I'm horribly afraid that the main reason I have never holidayed in a remote, unspoilt part of the world is because I can't afford it. If I suddenly get rich, I plan to use a travel company with sound green credentials. I have never knowingly bought tropical hardwoods, but I don't know what my door and window frames are made of – they'd been there for about fifty years before I moved in.

I grumble about clanking off to the bottle bank, but I do it. Any time now the local council is going to set up newspaper and can banks (for all kinds of cans which they plan to sort later by sliding them along a conveyor belt with a giant magnet suspended over it). So very shortly I shall be able to grumble about taking those along, as well.

I do have a shopping bag, but the occasional plastic carrier bag full of shopping does sometimes seem to leap out and attach itself to me. I've never owned a car, but I shouldn't be smug about that because I happily accept lifts from friends who do.

As my light bulbs give out, I'm replacing them with low-energy ones, and I'm training myself to lower the central heating thermostat. Every time I switch on the washing machine I feel guilty – despite the full load and the phosphate-free powder! – because there is a 78-year-old woman in the area who puts all her sheets in a bathful of soapy water and stamps on them rather than switch on hers. I am guiltily aware that I am using electricity even as I write this on the word processor, but the paper is recycled and I do re-use envelopes.

There is recycled lavatory paper in the bathroom, and nine times out of ten I turn off the tap while I clean my teeth. I admit there are more jars and bottles in there than necessary, but the stuff in them is all cruelty-free, and I was put off fur (except on live animals) when I was about six and discovered what my grandmother's winter coat was made of. Also, my great-aunt had a fox fur with a leather nose and a peg attachment where its mouth would have been so it could hang around her shoulders biting its own tail. To me, the ultimate horror was its glass eyes – I thought they were its real ones, preserved in some way. (If you're going to wear a dead animal, why stop short at the eyes?)

I've eaten less and less meat over the years and now don't eat any, but do eat fish. I quite often buy organic veg, and always free range eggs, usually from a local shop where I also get green household stuff. I re-use plastic food pots for storing leftovers. A compost heap is not practical on a balcony, so I waste all the vegetable stalks and peelings, but I deserve some credit for combating the recent plague of vine weevils with some extremely-organic nematodes. In my opinion, it takes nerve to accept delivery of five million parasitic worms and then stir them up in a bucket. However, I drop a huge number of points for losing concentration in the garden centre and buying a pack of peat-pots. I still don't believe I did that.

I would like to belong to almost all of the environmental organisations in the Address List, but that's not practical. For some years I've belonged to two international ones and one local one.

Before I worked on this book I thought of myself as a kind of mid-green – now I realise I wasn't as green as I thought I was and I am trying to improve (first step was to mail-order a loo-dam to conserve water and a string bag to keep the plastic ones at bay!).

The Artist (Martin Brown):
I'd like to say that, these days, I'm fairly green. I'd like to say that, but I don't think I am. I do all the easy stuff. I make sure all paper (not just newspapers) goes for recycling. Even the various manuscripts for this book will go to the paper bin or end up as note pads. All glass goes to the bottle bank. I use recycled paper – writing and loo. I also recycle as much as possible myself, whether it be cans into pencil holders or coat hangers into lampshades. I try to keep packaging down to a minimum, who wants carrots cling-film wrapped into their own dinky box anyway. I do eat meat, not a lot, but I do, though I try to ensure it is all from well-kept stock. I've never been keen on tropical hardwoods and I don't have a garden to garden in. I'm fairly good with water, coming from Australia where your dad drills saving water into your head from an early age (we even put bricks into the cistern of the loo to reduce the volume of the flush). I have a washing machine and a car. The car doesn't get used much, it just sits in the drive, gathers moss and annoys the neighbours. It's very small and if I washed it, it would be red. I use my bicycle a lot and my bathroom is pretty spartan.

When it comes to support for green issues I'm only OK. I support Greenpeace and Friends of the Earth. I care passionately about most things green, especially endangered species, not just the big well-known ones like tigers and rhinos, but the little obscure animals that nobody gets to hear of like the banded duiker and the giant earwig. However, I'm not so good at getting out there and campaigning. All word and no action?

As far as my work is concerned, the news is even less sparkling. All the drawings for this book were done on 200gsm A4 cartridge paper, wood-based, I think, and certainly bleached. Some of the best papers are fabric-based

161

but they are a lot more expensive of course. I don't know about the greenness of the pens I use, though the ink is water-based. Most of the pigments for my watercolours are chemical-based. The really bad news is about the brushes. The best watercolour brushes you can buy are sable. And the best sable you can get is a by-product of the fur industry. What is worse is that the sables are trapped from the wild. (I don't know if they are 'live' traps or leg traps.) There are alternatives. You can get a mixture of man-made fibre and sable or purely man-made fibre, but they are nowhere near as good. I'm still looking for a brush with the painting and water-holding qualities of sable, but until then I'm only bottle-bank and paper-bin green.

The Designer
(Clair Staniforth):
This is a tough one . . . I think the greenest thing I have ever done is to design this book. Since reading it, my eyes have been opened to a lot of issues that, until now, I have been unaware of – or maybe (like many other people) I was content *not* knowing the extent of damage that we cause our planet. Somehow, ignorance always seems to be the easy way out.

Having recently got engaged to a New Zealander (who, as a race, generally seem to have a very green outlook on life), I have learnt a few things that when incorporated in our everyday lives would make a difference. However small, I have now learnt that it *is* worth doing!

I cannot clean my teeth nowadays while the tap is still running, because of the guilty feeling of watching all that clean water go to waste. I save all bottles and newspapers and take them to the local recycling bins, instead of adding them to the ever-growing mountain of rubbish that is thrown out each week. I buy CFC-free deodorants and household products when possible, although I do feel that I could try a bit harder. I put the empty bottles out for the milkman . . . OK . . . OK . . . so does everyone else, but it still counts! Also, I have put a weighted bottle inside the toilet cistern to reduce the amount of water that is used with every flush.

So, having thought that I was probably the most ungreen person on the planet, I find that I do do small things, which, if everyone did, would probably make a considerable amount of difference. But I could definitely try a *lot* harder than I do . . . I think I'll go back to Chapter 1!

The Editor (Kate Petty):
A bit shaming, I'm afraid, apart from being responsible for various green publications . . . However, I am a lifelong vegetarian and my son and daughter are fourth-generation vegetarians, so as a family I like to think we've spared a few animal lives. And no hamburgers with all their ungreen connotations for us. We always check ingredients of food and cosmetics to make sure they don't contain animal products and haven't been tested on animals.

We take our bottles to the bottle bank and our newspapers to be recycled, and I have always passed on clothes and toys that the children have grown out of. We use recycled loo-paper (always bothers me, that phrase), kitchen roll, writing paper, etc, and I'm quite good about saying no to plastic carrier bags. Those that do turn up are used to line wastepaper baskets and for carrying swimsuits and towels when going swimming.

We all take showers far more often than we have baths, and the washing machine and dishwasher (oh dear) at least run full loads. We dry clothes outside and only use the tumbledryer (it gets worse) as a last resort. I seem to spend my whole time when I'm at home turning lights off, but I do try. I also prefer big jerseys and hot-water bottles to an overheated house.

We do have a car, but the kids have to walk to school or go on the bus. We did have it converted to take unleaded petrol, and we try not to use it unnecessarily – and again, with a full load when possible.

Oh, yes – and I have always cut up the plastic rings that hold six-packs together before throwing them away since I heard how much damage they do to wildlife.

That's about it. Definitely

could do better, I reckon.

The Paperback Publisher
(Caroline Thomas):
This is going to make me feel guilty.

First the good side . . .

I've never used aerosols and I always use 'good' washing powder, cleaners and washing-up liquid (I don't know why they're good, though – I just trust the labels). I try only to have a light on in the room in which I actually am. I buy recycled loo rolls and free range eggs. I buy lots of clothes secondhand and I save all my jars and make lots of pickles and preserves which I use as Christmas presents and supplies for me. I take all my other bottles to the bottle bank. I also make my own food as much as possible – my own pasta, mustard, soft cheese, flavoured oils, beansprouts, mayonnaise, soups, ice creams, jams, etc. (can't make bread, though) and I always buy my basic ingredients as unpackaged as possible, and in large bulk. I always refuse extra wrapping in shops and I make my own cards and wrapping paper (sometimes . . .). I use a string bag which folds up really small, and I always carry it in my bag (in an ideal world . . . what are all those plastic carrier bags doing in my house then?). Where possible I buy other products secondhand. I use the back of old manuscripts to write letters on (when they're not too official), and I don't own a car. I cycle as much as possible or use public transport. I try to avoid any unnecessary bathroom gumph and my cosmetics consist of four items: shampoo, conditioner, deodorant, moisturiser. I don't buy ivory, coral, shell or bone jewellery or souvenirs even when I'm really tempted. I give some of my income each month to Greenpeace, Survival International, Ranfurly Library (which recycles text and reading books to developing countries) and some other charities.

However . . .

I use a washing machine a lot (though at least always a full load . . .) and I have an ungreen fridge. I never think about conserving water nor, very much, about what sort of wood I buy. If someone pointed out to me that I was buying a tropical hardwood, I'd avoid it but I never think to ask. I don't own a battery charger and my lightbulbs are just ordinary ones. I have a spare bedroom in my house which makes me feel guilty, though I do make it available if anyone needs a place for a few weeks. I don't buy kindly meat when I buy meat and I have been known to eat foie gras (this is getting painful) though I never eat veal or frog's legs (who wants to?). I love going to developing countries on holiday and I haven't really thought about what I'm doing there. I could recycle my paper and cans but I don't. And probably worst of all: I'm building up a beautiful little back garden at the expense of all sorts of other environments and not thinking about it at all. I buy peat, I buy slug pellets, I buy plant foods without checking them, and I buy spring bulbs without being sure they haven't been ripped out of the Turkish countryside. I'm now feeling so bad about this that I promise to reform from now.

The Hardback Publisher
(Julia MacRae):
Green behaviour? Oh dear. My problem is partly generation gap. At 58, I am much older than the other partners in this book, and over the last few years I've had to undergo a pretty major attitude change. I grew up in Australia, at a time when we were all gloriously carefree and gave hardly a thought to the future of our planet. Wrong, yes, but at the time we didn't know it was wrong. It was not an issue, and we were simply not aware. We had sunshine, space, blue skies and a unique landscape to enjoy – and we thought it would last for ever. Sometimes there was a drought and water was short; rather more frequently bushfires devastated the countryside, leaving only burnt-out stumps where once had stood majestic native trees. But Nature took care of this, and we saw those blackened stumps miraculously regenerate, sprouting green shoots which quickly covered the scars of the fire. That, we thought in our innocence and unawareness, was how it would always be – Nature would take care of things.

But I am older now, and a

little wiser, and a lot more aware, because in the intervening years we have come to our senses and we now know that Man can destroy Nature beyond the point of regeneration, and with that realisation has come the need to change and adapt long-established living patterns. It's not easy to change: old habits die hard. I can't pretend I'm always good about it. I'm better in the garden than the house because I find it hard to kill any living creature, even the dreaded greenfly. I always use environmentally friendly garden preparations. I try to grow my own vegetables organically, but if I'm really honest I have to admit that this is mainly because the flavour is so much better. One of my greatest gardening joys was to find a family of hedgehogs thriving – hedgehogs, they say, like untidy gardens! Gardens should be places where wildlife can flourish, though it's not always easy to be charitable to squirrels.

I only use unleaded petrol and my car has a catalytic converter; I'm not entirely sure what this does, but anything which helps to reduce pollution in cities is worth trying. (It would be more to the point if I didn't use the car . . .)

In supermarkets, I don't actively shop green, but I do spend what seems like a very long time studying the labels and avoiding additives. I enjoy cooking and use mostly wholefood and natural ingredients. I don't use canned or frozen food unless I have frozen it myself. But then I guiltily remember that I am a working woman and can afford to buy fresh and/or organic produce, a privilege not to be taken for granted.

I am dreadful in the house. I simply don't think when I use the washing machine or the dishwasher. I do keep the heating at a low level (to the discomfort of some of my friends) and try to switch off lights. Like many Australians, I bath and shower rather more than is probably necessary – that's hot-climate conditioning in youth – but I'm ashamed to say that I slosh into the bath all manner of frothy stuff. And then I recoil in horror when I see all that same frothy stuff polluting and destroying our rivers and waterways. There is often hypocrisy in my attitude and writing this piece has brought this home to me. No, I don't wear fur or buy ivory or consciously support any organisation which profits from abuse of any living creature, but it's not enough just to be high-minded, and I realise I've got a lot more changing to do.

The Agent (Pat White):
How green is my patch?

The gardening bit of my life is pretty entrenchedly ecologically friendly. I use horse manure rather than any of the commercial fertilisers, although sometimes curse the grass seeds which accompany it. Country friends kindly bring me easily accessible manure – only once has someone managed to leave it on the train from Dorset!

I use soapy water to discourage greenfly, which works if you spray from the first signs of infestation. Can make the garden a bit foamy after a rainstorm. If the plague is intense and I have to use chemicals, I use selective killers which keep the ladybirds alive. After a frightening incident with slug pellets and a dog, I now use beer in saucers to trap slugs. A waterbutt collects run-off water from the garage roof, but I plumbed it in myself and it also fountains astonishingly in a downpour – definitely not according to instructions.

I do pick up after my dogs, binning it in council dog-waste bins. I wish there were bins, intelligently stationed, in more parks. In my part of London, the Pro-dog Brigade has badges saying, 'Carry Your Poop Scoop with Pride.'

Recycling of glass jars is a way of life. Friends who donate empties get home-made jams, jellies or pickles back. Barter always was a satisfactory way of life.

In a Perfect World, dustbin collection would allow for recycling from home, so no one had to take a car to a recycling centre. Tour buses would be precluded from idling their engines for hours on end while awaiting the return of passengers from tourist havens. Pump aerosols would never clog up. My pampered family of ladybirds would actually consume all the greenfly in my garden – and develop a taste for blackfly as well.

Chapter Twenty-one

IS THIS THE END?

Of the book? Yes. Of the world? No, not yet.

There is still time. The planet is self-healing – up to a point and given a chance. It shouldn't be beyond our ability to change our lifestyles enough to give it that chance. It shouldn't be impossible for us to solve the problems we've created.

After all, problem-solving is our thing – though it would be nice if we could refine our technique so that we didn't create three new ones each time we solved an old one.

On second thoughts, it was probably problem-solving that created most of the problems.

Problem-solving and the population explosion.

> "Overpopulation is our biggest problem today but nobody addresses it because it touches on religion and politics. We're breeding like rabbits on this planet. We don't have the resources to provide for everyone." Olivia Newton-John in *Hello* (9 January 1993)

Problem-solving, the population explosion and sleepwalking.

Arguably the single most useful thing any one person can do is wake up. Really wake up. Not just respond to the alarm-clock by opening the eyes and moving about.

Most of us are sleepwalking

most of the time, blankly following patterns of behaviour, forgetting that what we think of as the normal world is in fact a very recent invention. Sleepwalkers never think about the consequences of their actions because sleepwalkers never think.

It's more demanding, being awake, but far more interesting. Awake, we can see that the problems are not simple, but complex and interrelated and often quite tricky. But that's all right because, awake, we can cope with complexity.

Awake, it's possible to see that what works in one place may not work in another – that the dangers from industries vary – that all countries, whether developing or so-called developed are different – that things change all the time – that what works well today may or may not work so well tomorrow.

Awake we can adapt to the changing world.

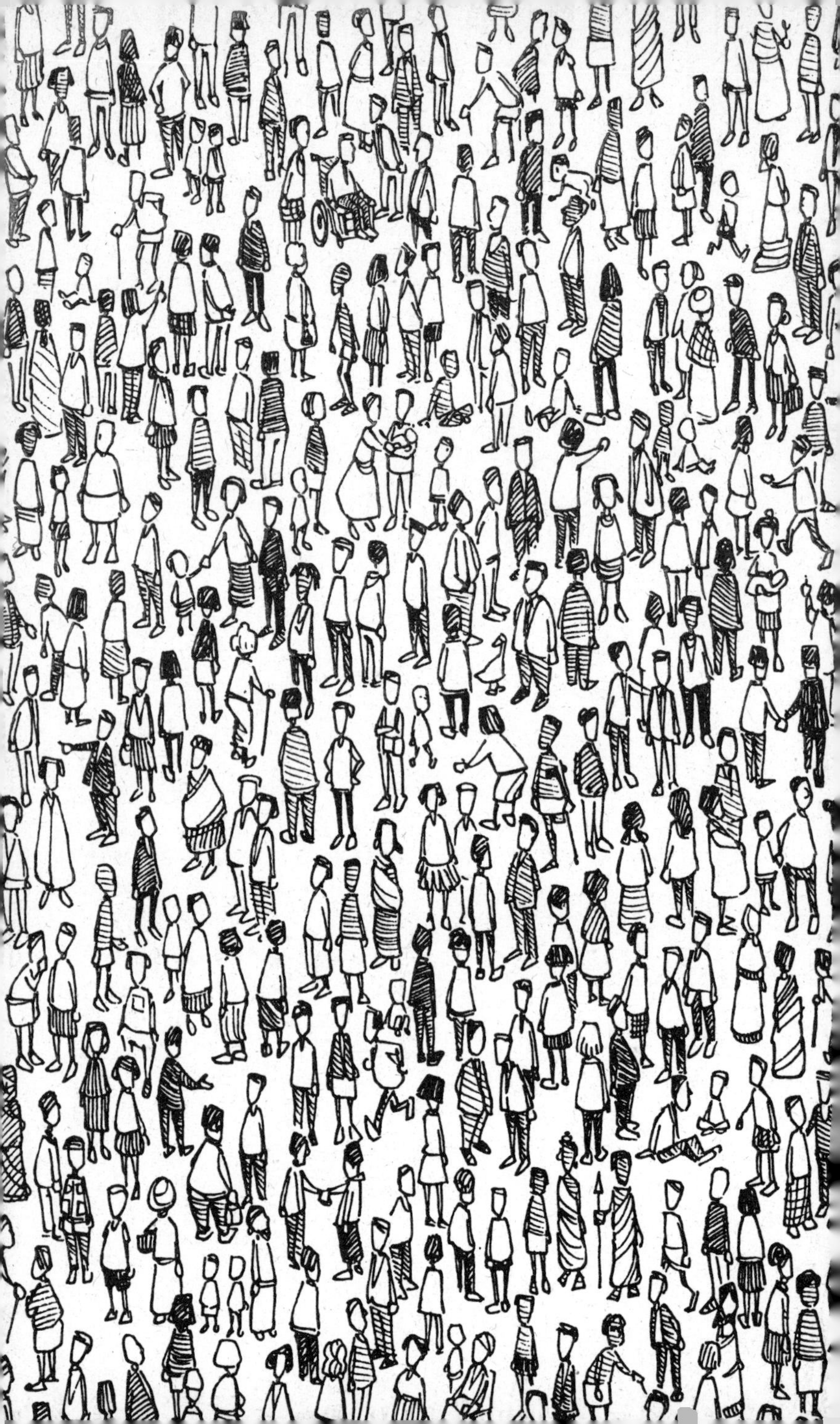

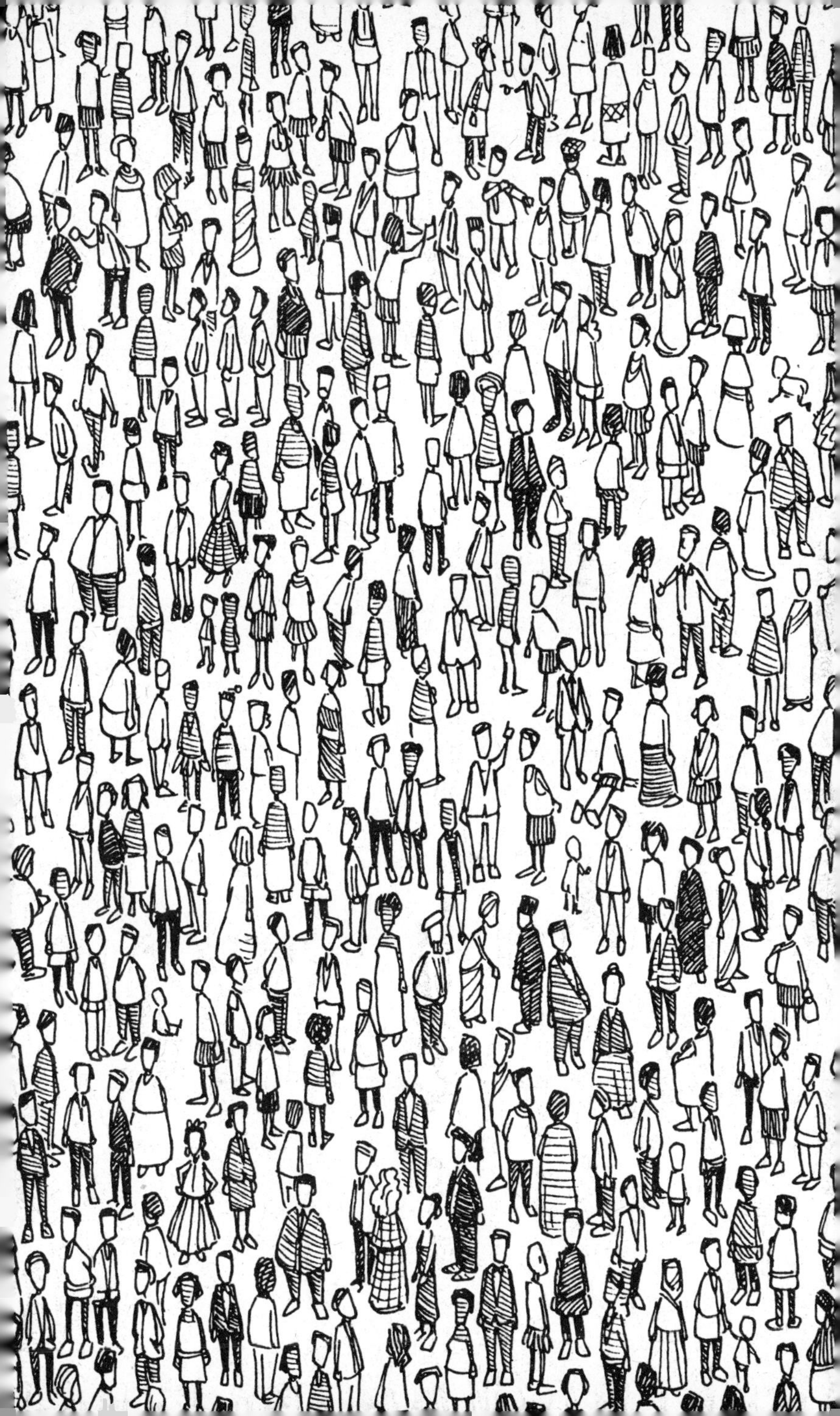

Any one of us alive on earth now must have descended, through the millenia, from the earliest life-forms of all. Whether you believe your most distant ancestors were Adam and Eve or uni-celled fungus-related blobs of gelatinous gunge, you have come far, adapting all along the line. If your ancestors hadn't adapted, you wouldn't be here. To stop adapting now would be such a waste of all those aeons of effort.

> "The dinosaurs didn't die out, they adapted and developed into birds. Who knows, with a bit of effort perhaps mankind will succeed in adapting and developing into human beings." Anon

To be fair, we'll never know if our distant ancestors were awake or not. It's more than likely that the early blobs of fungus-related gelatinous gunge just muddled through. But then the early blobs of gunge didn't invent PVC or the internal combustion engine or nuclear reactions or plastic carrier bags with the names of shops printed on them in toxic dye. So it wasn't as important for them to pay attention as it is for us.

It can be done.

The majority of environmentalists seem to be awake most of the time (though it must be said that politicians don't always see this as a plus).

> "If the troubles from environmentalists can't be solved in the jury box or at the ballot box perhaps the cartridge box should be used." James Watt, former US Interior Minister, quoted in *Green Magazine* (February 1993)

Some of the economists have recently woken and realised that it no longer makes sense to measure the economic state of a country solely in terms of GDP (Gross Domestic Product: the sum of all goods and services produced in that country) without taking natural resources into account.

> "A country can cut down its forests, erode its soils, pollute its aquifers and hunt its wildlife and fisheries to extinction, but its measured income is not affected as these assets disappear. Impoverishment is taken for progress." Robert Repetto, World Resources Institute at Washington DC, writing in the *Scientific American* (June 1992)

Even a few politicians have

begun to yawn and rub their eyes – though they're likely to need some hard kicks from the electorate to stop them dropping off again.

> "If I ruled the planet I would give all politicians a course in how to take care of the environment." Marte Graff Jenssen, 15, Norway

One final thought – the things which have gone wrong are not your fault, but starting to get them right is definitely in your interests!

ADDRESS LIST

There are more than 7,500 organisations of people who care either about the entire environment or about some specific aspect of it. It is not possible to list them all, so here are a few crucial addresses:

READ THIS LINE! When writing to ask any of these organisations for information, PLEASE ALWAYS ENCLOSE A LARGE STAMPED ADDRESSED ENVELOPE OR A SELF-ADDRESSED LABEL AND SOME STAMPS. THANK YOU.

GENERAL

Ark Environmental Foundation, 8-10 Bourdon St, London W1X 9HX. 071 409 2638. Seeks to educate people about their personal impact on the natural world; advises on products with low environmental impact.

Campaign for Nuclear Disarmament (CND), 162 Holloway Road, London N7 8DQ. 071 700 2350.

Centre for Alternative Technology, Machynlleth, Powys, SY20 9AZ. 0654 702400. Visits, courses, information leaflets on related subjects.

Earthkind, Avenue Lodge, Bounds Green Rd, London N22 4EU. 081 889 1595. Works through education and legislation to promote environmental responsibility and animal welfare.

Environmental Information Service, PO Box 197, Cawston, Norfolk, NR10 4BH. 0603 871048. Acts as a central clearing house to assist in locating groups, organisations and individuals involved with the environmental movement. Can assist schools and others to find organisations with the resources to deal with their queries.

Friends of the Earth (FoE), 26-28 Underwood St, London N1 7JU. 071 490 1555. One of the leading international environmental pressure groups, concerned with pollution, habitat destruction, energy issues, recycling. Also in: Argentina, Australia, Austria, Bangladesh, Belgium, Benin, Brazil, Bulgaria, Burkina Farso, Canada, Chile, Costa Rica, Curaçao (Antilles), Cyprus, Denmark, Ecuador, El Salvador, Estonia, France, Georgia, Germany, Ghana, Grenada, Hong Kong, Indonesia, Ireland, Italy, Japan, Latvia, Luxembourg, Malaysia, Malta, Netherlands, New Zealand, Nicaragua, Norway, Papua New Guinea, Paraguay, Philippines, Poland, Portugal, Scotland, Sierra Leone, Slovakia, Spain, Sweden, Tanzania, Togo, Ukraine, United States, Uruguay.

Gaia Foundation, 18 Well Walk, London NW3 1LD. 071 4355000. Works to promote ecological and cultural diversity and greater understanding between the Northern and Southern hemispheres.

Green Party, 10 Station Parade, Balham High Rd, London SW12 9AZ. 081 673 0045. Political party. There are also Green Parties in: Albania, Australia, Austria, Azerbaijan, Belgium, Bolivia, Brazil, Bulgaria, Canada, Chile, Denmark, Egypt, Estonia, Finland, France, Georgia, Germany, Greece, Hungary, Iceland, India, Ireland, Italy, Ivory Coast, Japan, Korea, Latvia, Lebanon, Lithuania, Luxembourg, Malta, Mexico, Mongolia, Netherlands, New Zealand, Norway, Peru, Philippines, Poland, Portugal, Romania, Russia, Slovenia, Spain, Sweden, Switzerland, Turkey, United States, Ukraine, Uruguay, Zaire, Zambia.

Greenpeace UK, Greenpeace House, Canonbury Villas, London N1 2PN. 071 354 5100 or 071 359 7396. Uses non-violent direct action and political lobbying, backed up by scientific research, to protest against/prevent destruction of wildlife and the environment. Also in: Argentina, Australia, Austria, Belgium, Brazil, Canada, Chile, Denmark, Finland, France, Germany, Greece, Guatamala, Ireland, Italy, Japan, Luxembourg, Netherlands, New Zealand, Norway, Russia, Spain, Sweden, Switzerland, Tunisia, Ukraine, United States.

Living Earth Foundation, The Old Laundry, Ossington Buildings, Moxon St, London W1M 3JD 071 487 3661. Important information and educational resource for schools (eg: Rainforest Resource Pack, Greensight, etc).

London Ecology Centre, 45 Shelton St, Covent Garden, London WC2 9HJ. 071 379 4324. Information resource, including information from environmental organisations, exhibitions.

Oxfam, 274 Banbury Rd, Oxford OX2 7DZ. 0865 312385. Concerned with long-term sustainable development in the Third World and also environmental issues such as deforestation, soil erosion and pollution.

Population Concern, 231 Tottenham Court Road, London W1P 9AE. 071 631 1546. Independent charity with UK education programme and development programmes in Africa, Asia, the Caribbean and Latin America. Information packs available.

Woodcraft Folk, 13 Ritherdon Rd, London SW17 8QE. 081 672 6031 or 081 767 2457. National voluntary youth organisation. Local groups for children – interest in global issues.

World Development Movement, 25 Beehive Place, London SW9 7QR. 071 737 6215. Campaigns against Third World poverty – ("Don't take pity, take action").

POLLUTION
Atmospheric Research and Information Centre, Department of Environmental Sciences, Manchester Metropolitan University, Chester St, Man-

chester M1 5GD. 061 247 1592. Researches into urban air quality, with special reference to acid rain and the greenhouse effect.

Campaign for Lead Free Air (CLEAR), 3 Endsleigh St, London WC1H 0DD. 071 387 4970.

National Society for Clean Air and Environmental Protection, 136 North St, Brighton BN1 1RG. 0273 26313. Members have access to library, journals and teaching packs.

Roopers Ltd, PO Box 82, Tunbridge Wells, Kent, TN3 8BZ. Sells Acid Drops Kit to test for Acid Rain.

RECYCLING

Aluminium Can Recycling Association (ALCAN), I-MEX House, 52 Blucher St, Birmingham B1 1QU. 021 633 4656. Advice on collecting and selling on.

Aluminium Foil Recycling Campaign, 38 High Street, Bradford-on-Avon, Warks, B50 4AA. 0800 626287. Aims to work with local authorities to set up recycling schemes. Information available.

Charities Aid Foundation, 48 Pembury Rd, Tonbridge, Kent, TN9 2JD. 0732 771333. "One man's rubbish is another man's treasure!" Compiles reasonably priced list of charities keen to acquire specific items.

Community Recycling Opportunities Programme, 7 Burner's Lane, Kiln Farm, Milton Keynes, MK11 3HA. 0908 562466. Encourages people to get together to raise money through recycling.

Steel Can Recycling Information Bureau, 69 Monmouth Street, London WC2H 9DG. 071 379 1306. Schools pack and information sheets available.

Tidy Britain Group, The Pier, Wigan, Lancs WN3 4EX. 0942 824620. Education pack for schools, information service for young people.

Wastewatch, Hobart House, Grosvenor Place, London SW1X 7AE. 071 245 9718. Organises community-based recycling and reclamation schemes. Local organisations. Guide to recycling waste.

OCEANS

Marine Conservation Society, 4 Gloucester Rd, Ross-on-Wye, Herefordshire HR9 5BU. 0989 66017. Concerned with the oceans and everything that lives in them.

Surfers Against Sewage, The Old Counthouse Warehouse, Wheal Kitty, St Agnes, Truro, Cornwall, TR5 0RE. 0872 553001. Pressure group fighting sea pollution.

COUNTRYSIDE
Association for the Protection of Rural Scotland, 14a Napier Rd, Edinburgh, EH10 5AY. 031 229 1898.

Campaign for the Protection of Rural Wales, Ty Gwyn, 31 High St, Welshpool, Powys SY21 7JP. 0938 552525.

Council for the Protection of Rural England, Warwick House, 25 Buckingham Palace Rd, London SW1W 0PP. 071 976 6433. Local branches.

National Trust, 36 Queen Anne's Gate, London SW1H 9AS. 071 222 9251. Looks after places of historic interest or natural beauty – major British landowner. (National Trust for Scotland, 5 Charlotte Sq, Edinburgh EG2 4OU. 031 226 5922.)

Rambler's Association, 1-5 Wandsworth Rd, London SW8 2XX. 071 582 6878. Seeks to protect footpaths, rights of way, woodlands, hedgerows – campaigns against use of pesticides in farming. Local branches organise walks.

WATCH Trust for Environmental Education, The Green, Witham Park, Waterside South, Lincoln LN5 7JR. 0522 544400. Junior wing of the UK Wildlife Trusts Partnership. Promotes environmental education and involvement with young people. Will supply the address of your local Wildlife Trust.

FLORA AND FAUNA (see also WILDLIFE)
Fauna and Flora Preservation Society, 1 Kensington Gore, London SW7 2AR. 071 823 8899. Major international conservation charity working with endangered species and habitats, mostly overseas.

International Tree Foundation, Sandy Lane, Crawley Down, West Sussex RH10 4HS. 0342 712536. Campaigns to save or replant trees, forests and woodlands worldwide.

Woodland Trust, Autumn Park, Dysart Rd, Grantham, Lincs, NG31 6LL. 0476 74297. Acquires, manages and conserves and replants broad-leaved and native woods in Britain.

WILDLIFE IN GENERAL
Born Free Foundation, Coldharbour, Dorking, Surrey RH5 6HA. 0306 712091. Founded as Zoo Check. Works to protect wildlife and wildlife habitats and to end the abuse and suffering of captive animals.

Local Wildlife Trusts: addresses available from WATCH above.

Royal Society for the Protection of Birds, The Lodge, Sandy, Beds, SG19 2DL. 0767 680551. Also runs a Young Ornithologists' Club, same address.

Scottish Wildlife Trust, Cramond House, Cramond Glebe Rd, Edinburgh,

EH4 6NS. 031 312 7765. For the protection of all types of wildlife in Scotland.

Wildlife Hospital Trust, 1 Pembleton Close, Aylesbury, Bucks, HP21 7NY. 0296 29860. Nurses injured birds and animals, especially hedgehogs.

WWF (UK), (World Wide Fund For Nature), Panda House, Weyside Park, Godalming, Surrey. 0483 426444. Largest private international conservation organisation with 28 affiliated and associated organisations around the world. Aims to conserve nature by reduction of pollution and of the wasteful consumption of resources. Special membership for young people.

SPECIFIC ANIMALS, BIRDS ETC

Bat Conservation Trust, c/o The Conservation Foundation, 1, Kensington Gore, London SW7 2AR. 071 240 0933. Educational materials available. Also has Young Batwatcher Club for under 16s.

British Hedgehog Preservation Society, Knowbury House, Knowbury, Ludlow, Shropshire SY8 3LQ. 0584 890287. Supply education pack for schools, and leaflets on all aspects of a hedgehog's life and needs.

Elefriends: see Born Free Foundation. Raises funds for anti-poaching initiatives and campaigns against the sale of ivory.

International Dolphin Watch, Parklands, North Ferriby, Humberside, HU14 3ET. 0482 643403.

National Federation of Badger Groups, 16 Ashdown Gardens, Sanderstead, South Croydon, Surrey, CR2 9DR. Will put you in touch with your nearest badger group.

Orkney Seal Rescue, Dyke End, South Ronaldsay, Orkney KW17 2IJ. 0856 83463.

Otter Trust, Earsham, Nr Bungay, Suffolk NR35 2AF. 0986 893470. Breed otters for release into the wild and maintain two reservations. For information on otters in a specific location, contact local Wildlife Trust.

Whale and Dolphin Conservation Society, Alexander House, James St West, Bath, Avon, BA1 2BT. 0225 334511. Most popular money-raising venture so far? The Adopt a Whale or Dolphin scheme!

DOMESTIC, LABORATORY AND FARM ANIMALS

Animal Aid (including Youth Section), 7 Castle St, Tonbridge, Kent TN9 1BH. 0732 364546. Increases awareness of abuse of animals in vivisection and factory farming.

British Union for the Abolition of Vivisection (BUAV), 16a Crane Grove, London N7 8LB. 071 700 4888. Approved product guides

Chickens' Lib, PO Box 2, Holmfirth, Huddersfield HD7 1QT. Leaflets, stickers, posters and videos.

Compassion in World Farming (including youth group called Farm Animal Rangers), 5a Charles St, Petersfield, Hants, GU32 3EH. 0730 264208. Britain's leading farm animal welfare organisation, campaigning against factory farming and the live animal export trade.

Fund for the Replacement of Animals in Medical Experiments (FRAME), Eastgate House, 34 Stoney St, Nottingham NG1 1NB. 0602 584740. Education packs, product lists, regional meetings.

National Anti-Vivisection Society (Junior Section called Animals' Defenders), 261 Goldhawk Rd, London W12 9PE. 081 846 9777.

Rare Breeds Survival Trust, 4th St, National Agricultural Centre, Stoneleigh, Kenilworth, Warwickshire CV8 2LG. 0203 696551.

Respect for Animals, PO Box 500, Nottingham NG1 3AS. 0602 525440. Has taken up the anti-fur campaign following the demise of Lynx. Further campaigns are planned to destroy the markets for products of cruelty to animals.

Royal Society for the Prevention of Cruelty to Animals (RSPCA), The Causeway, Horsham, West Sussex, RH12 1HG. 0403 64181. (Scottish Society for the Prevention of Cruelty to Animals, 19 Melville St, Edinburgh EH3 7PL. 031 225 6418.)

CIRCUSES AND ZOOS
Captive Animals Protection Society, 36 Braemor Court, Kingsway, Hove, East Sussex, BN3 4FG. 0273 737756. Concentrates on plight of circus animals.

Zoo Check: see Born Free Foundation.

ORGANIC FARMING AND GARDENING
Henry Doubleday Research Association, National Centre for Organic Gardening, Ryton-on-Dunsmore, Coventry, CV8 3LG. 0203 303517. Will supply garden needs by mail order via Chase Organics – see Green Mail Order.

National Federation of City Farms and Community Gardens, AMF House, 93 Whitby Rd, Brislington, Bristol BS4 3QF. 0272 719109. Will supply the address of your nearest City Farm or Community Garden.

Soil Association, 86 Colston St, Bristol BS1 5BB. 0272 290661. Promotes organic farming and food production and produces an education pack. Mail order catalogue for books.

TRANSPORT
Cyclists' Touring Club (International), Cotterell House, 69 Meadrow,

Godalming, Surrey, GU7 3HS. 0483 417217. Lobbies for improved road facilities for all cyclists. Members get technical advice on choosing and maintaining a cycle.

Transport 2000, Walkden House, 10 Melton St, London NW1 2EJ. 071 388 8386. Campaigns for environmentally friendly transport.

GREEN MAIL ORDER
Beauty without Cruelty, 57 King Henry's Walk, London N1 4NH. 071 254 2929. Educational trust – supplies information on avoiding fur, leather, silk and down (as in feathers) as well as cruelty-free list of cosmetic products.

Chase Organics (GB) Ltd, Addlestone, Surrey, KT15 1HY. 0932 820958. Mail order for gardening equipment, books, biological pest controls, peat-free compost etc.

"Choose Cruelty Free" Hotline: 071 700 4232. (Run by British Union for the Abolition of Vivisection.) Phone for list of acceptable products.

Cosmetics To Go, 0800 373 366. Freephone for wild and wonderful catalogue, all cruelty free.

The Green Catalogue, 3-4 Badgworth Barns, Notting Hill Way, Weare, Axbridge, Somerset BS26 2JU. 0934 732469. Mail order clothes, cosmetics, household stuff, can crushers etc. (mainly UK but also the rest of Europe).

Green Light, 11b High Street, Shepton Mallet, Somerset BA4 5AA. 0749 346135. Mail order supplier of all types of low energy light bulbs.

Traidcraft, Kingsway, Gateshead, Tyne and Wear, NE11 0NE. 091 491 0591. Sells Third World goods which have been imported at a fair price to the producer – in shops and via mail order catalogue – including food, household goods, presents, clothes.

Vegetarian Shoes, 12 Gardner Street, Brighton BN1 1UP. 0273 691913. Mail order of leather-free footwear.

See also merchandise catalogues available from many of the other organisations listed.

FOOD
Real Meat Company Ltd, Warminster BA12 0HR. 0985 840436. Independent company which promotes meat from animals reared without factory farming methods. Sells direct to customers (minimum order 5 kilos delivered to your door). Also supplies list of 'real meat' retailers and education packs.

Vegan Society, 7 Battle Rd, St Leonards-on-Sea, East Sussex, TN37 7AA.

0424 427393. Advocates a way of life which excludes all animal products. General information pack and cook books.

Vegetarian Society, Parkdale, Dunham Rd, Altrincham, Cheshire WA14 4QG. 061 928 0793. Also runs School Campaign for Reaction Against Meat (SCREAM). Resource pack for secondary schools, cookery courses, books leaflets etc.

HOLIDAYS AND TOURISM

British Trust for Conservation Volunteers, 36 St Mary's St, Wallingford, Oxfordshire, OX10 0EU. 0491 39766. Conservation holidays for 16+. Local group activities.

Field Studies Council, Central Services, Preston Montford, Montford Bridge, Shrewsbury, SY4 1HW. 0743 850674. Residential courses on environmental matters and wildlife.

Operation Raleigh, Raleigh International, Alpha Place, Flood St, London SW3 5SZ. 071 351 7541. Organises 10-11 week expeditions on community and conservation projects for 17-25s.

Tourism Concern, Froebel College, Roehampton Lane, London SW15 5PJ. 081 878 9053. Campaigns for just and sustainable tourism. Members have access to resource centre, information packs, books and videos.

INDEX

A

Acid deposition **27**, 28, 30, 32, 34
Acid rain 23, **26-34**, 49, 57, 64, 105
Adhesives 9
Aerosols 6, 8, 10, 80, 105
Aflatoxin 45
Agenda 21 **4**, 75
Agro-chemicals 36, 38, 63
Aid 16, 17, 65
Algae 36, 38, 72, 78, 97
Aluminium 27, 110, 111
Ammonia (NH_3) 28, 34
Animal testing 51-2, **55-6**, 90, 142, 150-1
Antarctic 5, 9, 11, 70
Aral Sea 40, 66
Arctic 5, 37
Arsenic 45
Australia 25, **63**

B

Bank, World 16
Batteries 45-6, 79, 105-7, 116, 121
Benzene C_6H_6 49, 112
Bhopal 43-4
Bicycles 64, **118**
Biodiversity & extinction 16, 19, 56-8, 67-8, 172
Bleach 36, 46-7, 78, 81, 83, 108, 142
Botulinum 45, 50
Brazil 17, 19, 69, 89
Brazil nuts 18, 19
Britain 16, 17, 28-9, 31, 34, 38-9, **60**, 70, 72
BSE 94
Burgers 100-1
Bush, George 12, 25

C

Cadmium **45**, 106-7
Cameras 127
Canada 16, **63-4**
Carbon cycle 21
Carbon dioxide (CO_2) 12, 13, 16, **20-2**, 24-5, **50**, 64, 72, 117-8
Carbon monoxide (CO) 34, 44, 49, **50**, 112, 118
Carbon tetrachloride 9
Cars, electric 67, **115-6**
Cars, petrol-driven 13, 22, 24, 33-4, 36, 49, 62, 72, **112-19**, 124
Catalytic converters 33, **116-7**
CFCs 6-11, 47, 72, 97, 100
Chemicals, natural & synthetic 44
Chernobyl 48
Chlorine 6, 8-11, 46-7, 108, 142
Chlorine gas 81
Chlorine nitrate ($ClONO_2$) 11
Cleaning (housework) 80-1
CNG 63, 65, **118-9**
Companion planting 131-3
Compost 97, 109-10, 136-7
Copper 89
Coral 63, 83, **87**, 125
Correcting fluids 9
Cosmetics 89-90
Cotton 83
Critical levels 31
Critical loads 30-1

D

Dams 19, 41, 69
Debt, Third World 13, 14-16
Denmark 60
Diamonds 88
Diesel fuel 118
Dioxins 47, 50, 108
Dodo 56
DOE 34, 112-3
Dolphins 95, 142-3
Domestic waste 36, 42, 60, 63, 76-7, 104-11
Draize test 52, **90**
Dry-cleaning 9, 79, 85-6
Dyes 9, 18, 78, 83

E

Earth Summit **3**, 4, 12, 24, 65, 67, 75
Ecological Trading Co 15, 18
Ecuador 15, 143
Energy, from fossil fuels 22, 28, 33, 48, 119-22
Energy, nuclear 48
Energy, renewable 20, 25, 60-5, 67, 74, 116, 121
Energy saving 34, 73, 79, 84, 108, 110, 121-2

E Numbers 97, **149-50**
Ethanol 116
Europe 25, 32, 37, **59-63**, 104
Eutrophication 30

F

Farming, intensive **93-6**, 144
Farming, organic 98, 147
Fertilisers 16, 22, 36, 39, 57, 60, 65, 83, 97, 137
Fish farms 96
Fish & fishing 31, 47, 65, 71, 95-6
Fossil fuels 13, 22, 23, 28, 33, 48, 119-22
France 60-1
Fridges 6, 8, 10, **11**, 71
Fungicides 97
Fur trade **53**, 58, 85-6

G

GATT 95
GDP 172
Genetic engineering 83, 98-100
Germany 16, 29, **61-2**, 71
Global Forum 3
Gold 46, 89
Green Con Awards 141, 147
Greenhouse effect 6, 10, 16, **20-5**, 49, 57, 66-7, 105
Greenhouse gases 6, 12, **20-1**, 23, 25, 100
Gulf War 40

H

Halon **9**, 11
Hazardous waste 37, 105, 106
HCFCs **8**, 9
Heavy metals 27, 39, 42, 45, 60, 106-7
Hedgehogs 74, 130, 134-35
Herbicides 97, 130
Hydrocarbons 22, 28, 48-9, 112, 118
Hydrochloric acid (HCl) 11
Hydro-electric plants 41

I

India 35, 43-4, 61, 74
Industrial Revolution 23, 27, 59
Industrial processes 13, 22, 24, 28, 33-4, 36, 41-2, 45, 48-9
Industrial waste 36, 39, 63
Infra-red 25
Insecticide 44, 47, 83
Irradiation 97-8
Ivory 88

J

Japan 58, **64-5**, 70
Jewellery 86-9

L

Labelling 90-1, 98, **139-51**
Landfills 22, 36, 44, 47, 105
Lavatory paper, 76-9
Leachate 36, 47
Lead 45, **46**, 81, 106, 118, 137
Leather/skins 58, 65, 86
Light bulbs 71
Lime & liming 31-4

M

Medicinal plants 18, 19, 56
Medicines 8, 18, 45-6, 52, 55-6, 105
Mendes, Chico 19
Mercury 45, **46**, 50, 81, 89, 106
Metals precious 13, 15, 46, 89
Methane (CH_4) 20-2, 48, 100, **105**
Methyl bromide **9**, 97
Methyl chloroform 9, 86
Methyl isocyanate 44
Montreal Protocol **7**, 8-10

N

NASA 5
Netherlands 10, 29, 40, **62**, 72
New Zealand 65-6
Nitrates 60, 147
Nitric acid trihydrate 11
Nitrogen 11, 28, 30-1
Nitrogen dioxide (NO_2) 11
Nitrogen oxides (NO_x) 26, 28, 33-4, 48-9, 112, 118
Nitrous oxides (N_2O) 20-2
NMVOCs 28, 34, 48
Norway 29, 31, 33, **62**
Nuclear power 48
Nuclear waste 37, 49, 66, 98, 105
Nuclear weapons 66

O

Oil 13, 40, 48, 84, 86
Oil spills 40, 48, 57
Oil tankers 40, 48
OPEC 13
Organic gardening & farming 61, 72, 98, **130-8**, 147
Organochlorine 47
Ozone (O_3) 6, 11, 20-2, 28, 34, 49, 147

183

Ozone layer **5-11**, 57, 64

P

Packaging 61, 81, 100, 102-5, 107-8
Paints 9, 47, 50, **81**, 105
Paraquat 130-1
PCBs 37, **47**
Peanut butter 45
Peat 30-1, 57, 75, 136
Peru 18
Pesticides 9, 36, 57, 65, 73, 83, 97, 98, 130
Petrol 46, 48, 72
pH scale **27-8**, 32
Philippines 17, 74
Phosphates 36, 79, 147-8
Photosynthesis 21
PICs 47-8
Plastics 37, 39, 46-8, 50, 72, 82, 108-9
Poland 35
Population 50, 168, 170-1
Potassium cyanide 89
Power stations 13, 22, 28, 33-4, 49
PSCs 11
Public transport 115, 119

R

Radioactive waste 37
Rainforests **12-19**, 56-7, 60, 63, 65, 69, 74, 100
Reagan, Ronald 12
Recycling 41, 60, 83-4, 100, 107-11
Rubber 18, 19
Rubbish 35-7, **104-11**
Russia 40, **66**

S

Scandinavia 28-9, 32-3
Seal death 39
Sewage 36-9, 42, 60, 63, 70, 73, 76-9, 105, 124
Shaving 79
Shells 87
Shire horses 71
Silage 36
Silk 83-4

Silver 89
Slash-and-burn 16
Slurry 36
Smog 6, 118
Soil 16, 30-1, 63, 65-6
Solar energy 20, 25
Solvents 28, 47, 49
Spain 62
Stain removers 9
Stockholm Conference 3
Stratosphere 5, 6, 8, 9, 20, 22
Sulphur 22-3, 28, 30, 33
Sulphur dioxide (SO_2) 22-3, 26, 28, 33-4, 48-50, 149
Sweden 31, 33, **63**
Synthetic fabrics 84, 86
Sustainable development 16-19

T

Titanium oxide 78, 81
Tobacco 45
Toothpaste 78
Toxic waste 37, 60-2, 66, 67, 72, 105-6
Tree death 32
Trichlorethan 1.1.1 9, 86
Tropical hardwoods 12-19, 60, 140-1

U

Ultraviolet radiation 6, 7, 11, 21, 23, 57, 63
United Nations 3, 35
UN Economic Commission 29
UN Environment Programme 7
US 16, 24, 25, **66-8**, 104

V

Vostock Ice Core 23

W

Washing powder/liquid 36, 79-80, 141-2
Water use 41, 61-4, 66-7, 76-8, 83, 88-9, 127, 129, 134-5, 137
Whales & Whaling 62, 65
Wool 83
Wormi doo 134

Z

Zinc 45, **46-7**, 89